AFTER A DANCE: Selected Stories

Bridget O'Connor was born in London in 1961, and began her career as a writer whilst working in a building-site canteen. In her spare moments she penned darkly comic and excruciatingly well-observed short stories, one of which, 'Harp', won the 1991 *Time Out* Short Story Prize. Two collections followed, *Here Comes John* (1993) and *Tell Her You Love Her* (1997).

In 2001 her stage play *The Flags* was performed at the Manchester Royal Exchange before being produced in Liverpool, Dublin, Belfast, Slovenia, and Australia. Like so much of her writing, it was praised as much for being 'sharp and gritty' as for its 'sublimely drawn' characters and situations (*The Guardian*).

As a screenwriter, Bridget often worked with her husband, Peter Straughan, and their final screenplay together was the Oscar-nominated and BAFTA-winning *Tinker Tailor Soldier Spy*. She once called herself a happy pessimist, and shining humour into dark corners was a speciality in her work and elsewhere.

Bridget died in 2010, and was survived by Peter and their daughter Constance.

By Bridget O'Connor

Here Comes John
Tell Her You Love Her
The Flags

Praise for Bridget O'Connor

'Wickedly funny, stylishly written, I relished each and every one of these stories'

Patrick McCabe, author of *The Butcher Boy*

'In this new collection her most accomplished and most devastating stories lie side by side. O'Connor writes of everyday characters so pitiful they are ridiculous, so awful they become lovable . . . The language is unexpected and the twists are often absurd. Reading O'Connor is always a delight'

New Statesman

'*Here Comes John* is a fictional whirlwind. O'Connor whisks us through a multiplicity of voices – an enraged wife who kills a purveyor of pornographic magazines; a twenty-five-year-old woman about to lose her teeth; a horribly capricious teenager who refuses to acknowledge her friend is HIV positive . . . O'Connor is at her nightmarish best here, the writing as tautly coiled as a thriller . . . [She] handles it with well-judged care and startling precision'

The Irish Times

'A master of the [short story]. The results are both vivacious and vicious. But even at their most painful, they sing'

The Herald

'Bridget O'Connor creates unforgettable voices. Sad, funny, disturbing, the tales in *After a Dance* are odd, and oddly luminous'

The Times Literary Supplement

'Every O'Connor story is a performance, a live fight with time and decay, disgust and the human body. She wrote intensely from her time and place; to read her now is to be catapulted back to 1990s London. Yet the voice, the themes are more relevant than ever. No wonder she was so preoccupied with temporality: she was before her time'

Martina Evans, *The Irish Times*

'O'Connor had a masterly ability to conjure the dark, the shady, even the repulsive side of people. Many of her characters are not particularly appealing. All of them, however, feel addictively real'

Literary Review

After a Dance

Stories

+

BRIDGET O'CONNOR

PICADOR

First published 2024 by Picador

This edition first published 2025 by Picador
an imprint of Pan Macmillan
The Smithson, 6 Briset Street, London EC1M 5NR
EU representative: Macmillan Publishers Ireland Ltd, 1st Floor,
The Liffey Trust Centre, 117–126 Sheriff Street Upper,
Dublin 1, D01 YC43
Associated companies throughout the world
www.panmacmillan.com

ISBN 978-1-0350-2486-5

These stories were previously published in *Here Comes John* (Jonathan Cape, 1993;
Picador, 1995) and *Tell Her You Love Her* (Picador, 1997). 'Heavy Petting' originally
appeared in *Intoxication: an anthology of stimulant-based writing*, edited
by Toni Davidson (Serpent's Tail, 1998). 'At least pull your jumper up'
originally appeared in *Five Dials*, number 24 (Hamish Hamilton, 2015).

1 3 5 7 9 8 6 4 2

A CIP catalogue record for this book is available from the British Library.

Typeset in Electra by Jouve (UK), Milton Keynes
Printed and bound by CPI Group (UK) Ltd, Croydon, CR0 4YY

Visit **www.picador.com** to read more about all our books
and to buy them. You will also find features, author interviews and
news of any author events, and you can sign up for e-newsletters
so that you're always first to hear about our new releases.

Contents

Introduction

My mother's grandmother – her namesake, Bridget O'Connor –
worked as a maid on an Irish estate. One day, a bull charged
at her master and she jumped over the fence with a pitchfork
and stabbed it to death. Every year afterwards, she was gifted
a flower to commemorate her courage. In 1993 she was given
a copy of her granddaughter's book of short stories, entitled
Here Comes John. It just so happens that the elder Bridget
O'Connor received a visit from the parish priest on the first
Friday of every month. On one of his trips she paid him to
say mass over the book, as a form of exorcism. Until then,
she sat on it, so that no one would see it. In an interview to
celebrate her debut, my mother was asked about her parents'
reactions. 'My mother said it was very poetical but she told
my brother she thought it was very boring . . . she said there's
enough swearing on buses and on the television.' The inter-
viewer noted: 'The author is disarmingly, if disconcertingly,
frank.'

The exorcised stories are filled with dark, cruel, lonely people, wandering around, lost. 'Selfish people attract me,' my mother once said, 'because they're not soaking up any experience, not really seeing anything.' There is often a gap between who the narrator thinks they are, and who we understand them to be. Funny, then, that all four of my mother's siblings were convinced that there was one story written about each of them. Tina, in 'I'm Running Late', who is too transfixed by her yellowing teeth to realize that her friend is telling her that she's HIV positive, 'is based on my sister Peggy actually.' She pops up again in the second collection – which takes its title from the time that Peggy's boyfriend asked my mother out for dinner in exchange for relationship advice. Only interested in the free meal, she said distractedly, 'Just tell her you love her.' Her sister Rosie inspired the conniving gold-digger in 'Here Comes John', and her brother James features as a best man on a bender in 'Love Jobs'. The stand out cameo, however, is her sister Kathleen, who was once given a goldfish by a boyfriend and, when they broke up, took to trying to stab the fish to death with a fork; which finds its way into 'Heavy Petting'.

My mother appears as herself in a series of comedy stories written for *The Irish Post* in which she plays a failing writer, as delusional as any of her characters. 'I looked in the mirror and told myself some lies whilst blinking. You have, I said, a new two-book deal. You have been shortlisted for the Orange Prize. All your rivals have died in a bloody skirmish at the

Arts Council whilst receiving prizes meant for you.' Real life and fiction continue to blur, even in her letters, which also exist in the world of story: there are enemies, friends, true loves. She's thrilled by her new word processor. She attends CND protests (for the cake). Princess Diana walks down her street. During the day she works at a bookshop on Muswell Hill – and the boredom inspires 'Shop Talk'. In her words, 'Nothing happens and yet the day has been packed with feeling.'

In her neighbourhood there are 'big trees and ten-year-old muggers.' Moving into a house with no lock on the front door, she writes: 'I foiled the burglar by putting up loads of bricks against the door and various sauce pans to trip over.' And then at an Abbey National cash machine she's robbed at knife point (a moment which is reanimated in 'Tell Her You Love Her'). Martina Evans writes about the incident in *The Irish Times*. She continues: 'I think of her every time I pass the Irish pub where Bridget once saw two nuns pulling pints behind the counter. She assured me they were not in fancy dress but family members helping out in an emergency. And they are as real in my imagination now as the Joycean barmaids in *Ulysses*, even though I never saw them and I'm still not sure Bridget wasn't pulling my leg.' When asked what the most overrated virtue is, my mother answered, 'Truth-telling.' Naturally, as she was following in the family footsteps of creative honesty (see: woman jumps over fence, kills bull). Once, during a maths exam, she filled in the paper with a tale about a monkey – she told me that she'd just felt that the story was more important.

There's body-horror, disgust, dirt and grime in the stories. Decay. Teeth and hair fall out, insects nest, time passes by furiously, things fall apart. Women and men stand on two different sides, and seem doomed never to understand the other. My mother was fascinated by the language of the men around her, and she often spoke through the male voice – 'My name's Tony Wornel, to cut a long story short' – and depicted men talking and drinking, hinting at things they can't say out loud. Whilst the stories are populated with male villains – creeping uncles, paedophilic teachers, a serial killer, 'the Wankers are everywhere' – it is the monstrous women that get you in the end.

The woman in 'Harp' strokes her victim's tear-streaked face, whilst the sugar baby in 'Here Comes John' describes gleefully entrapping men, who aren't people to her, just an 'it'. Meanwhile, Lucy, the celebrity cancer patient in 'Remission', has been dying publicly for six years, though our narrator begins to suspect that she is, in fact, immortal. The story pulls you one way, and then the other: 'He put his key in the lock and the house turned.' Even the stories she wrote for me as a child were subversive. (The moral: always be nice to the witch.) Her narrators often seem to be acting out revenge fantasies – dreaming about attacking predators, posh kids, people who don't love them any more. But in reality, the characters are paralysed, in her words, 'they long to escape, and they try to, but they eventually go nowhere.'

On first meeting my mother, her agent told her that there was one thing she couldn't work out. Are you an optimist or a pessimist? 'Happy pessimist,' she replied straight away. (In another piece for *The Irish Post* she writes: 'My positive attitude has been praised by the nuns at my old school . . . [they would say] "little Bridget makes the most of a bad job" and "fair play to the girl with the braces".') Martin Doyle, literary editor of *The Irish Times*, wrote that 'It certainly seems that for O'Connor there can be no love stories in this selfish, consumerist, unfaithful age. Ego has supplanted Eros as a subject of fascination.' This strikes me as ironic, as my mother was really very romantic. My parents had the kind of marriage that at the time I took for granted, but now realize is incredibly rare.

Whilst writing films together, they would disappear into their studies – my mother's at the back of the house, my dad's in the attic – and then come together to redraft. A mostly peaceful process (though once in a fight over a script, my mother reached over and spat into his glass of milk). She never considered screenwriting serious work. As my dad once wrote: 'Short stories were her first and enduring love. She worked on the movies because we enjoyed doing them together. And because she got to go to parties.' For their film *Tinker Tailor Soldier Spy*, she won posthumously two Baftas and was nominated for an Oscar.

I remember once, I was ushered out of the kitchen as my mother had just finished a story and she wanted to show it to my dad. Our kitchen door had a glass window, so I turned around and watched through it as he sat down with the laptop, and my mother hovered next to him, bouncing on the balls of her feet. She was so excited for him to read it.

Constance Straughan

Love Jobs

Here's him, Steve, laughing, the afternoon after, tearing and screwing up wrapping paper, missing the bin by three yards of carpet. So far they've got: one fondue set, one glass fish, two toasters, five sets of towels, three double duvet covers, a crystallized punch bowl, four sets of darts, two sets of guitar strings, one plectrum and not a lot else. Here's her, the bride, Gilly, diving at the papers, smoothing and folding them up, she's the kind that keeps. She's gone mad. They should have got a wedding list from a department store: they've got crap. She told him five, six, how many times? Her face is tight; her home-done highlights fly around the room like sparks. Here's me, the Best Man, death warmed up. I've slept in my tux. She yanks the cushion out from under my neck. Here's him, 'Hey more like it, *nice*, from Eve.' *Eve.*

He's holding up silver, a photo frame, he holds it up in a sun beam, it cuts right inside my eyes. My shattered eyes. He drops it: 'Oh, whoops.' She goes for him. I go for a walk.

As I go down the hall I hear her go, 'What's *he* still here for?'

As I click the gate I hear a muted thump, a toaster. I hear her go, 'You ruddy . . .'

I'm halfway down the road when it's panting: it's Steve with his dog. He's in his vest, boxers and a grin. He's pinned Gilly's wedding veil on, it's floating out. I hear her squeal, 'Bring that back . . . or . . .' Steve hands me Muttley like a bag. 'Take her walkies, Joey, or she'll kill it.' And he's backing up the road. And he's in the house. I think – married: that's my one mate gone; that's the end of that.

Here's me down on the tow-path, by the canal. It's not pretty. I'm standing on ginger leaves, flattened doggy-do. The sky is one low-down cloud of bilge smoke. The water is not water. It's black, still, Guinness, with oil on top of it, with dust on top of it, under it God knows, bicycle skeletons, skeletons. *Nothing* could live in that. If it wasn't so stinking I'd jump straight in. Here's me: hung over, hung right over. Some-where, further down, a generator is pounding at my head. I've got to find a dead quiet place, do a think about her, Eve, my ex-wife. I hadn't thought about her in . . . five years. We all used to gig together me, Steve, Eve: 'The Three Leaves'. I still can't believe . . . at the wedding, I still can't believe she just *walked past*. I've got to get home, get flat. I've got Mut-tley on the wanderlead. She's sniffing stuffed bin-liners, out on the slack. She crouches and strains and some dogs-do is so disgusting, it's hanging out like another tail, I can't look.

It's in the second I look away, out of nowhere, two blokes

in black. I'm going to get mugged. I think, who cares? Then it's like I'm taking photos, rapid, action shots. There's a fat one and a thin one. The thin one, he's got Muttley – click, and the fat one . . . he's got an iron bar – click, whacking it on his leg – click, charging up the tow-path – click click click. Here's the fat one: 'Oy, Tuxedo. Give,' rubbing his forefinger and thumb. The thin one holds Muttley up above the black. The extra tail is still there. I go, 'Yeah, or what?' I really don't care. 'Or the bitch gets it.' Here's me, my best shrug, 'So, she ain't my dog.' And Muttley's in. She plops in like a rock and don't come up. Not a ripple . . . The fat one goes, 'Oh bloody hell Neville,' . . . not for years. The thin one goes, 'She wriggled I . . .' And Muttley pops up, a flashy paddle to the other side. Halfway there she turns and doggy-grins. I doggy-grin back. Then her nails scratch bricks. She can't get out. The fat one goes, 'Look, she can't get out!' His voice squeaks up but I give a tug on the wanderlead and Muttley is back going yap yap. Here's me, I go, 'With your permission, gentlemen.' I haul her up. Snap. As I haul, this bone in her neck goes Snap, the littlest sound like snapping a twig, it don't seem enough, but Muttley is slack on the end of the line. Dead. Hanging there like a big furry fish. Dead. They look at me. It is quiet. Here's me, I can't believe this, I come undone, I start to bawl like a girl. I see red. I see Eve's dress. The fat one coughs, but I just can't stop. He lights three fags all together, goes, 'Honest mate, I'm real, real sorry.' The thin one goes, 'Yeah me too, Gord, a man's best friend . . . If I could turn the clock back . . .'

3

The first drink is elixir. Like drinking gold. Here's us sitting on a pigeon-slashed bench smoking the fags. A dirty swan is turning on the water, on rubbish. Muttley is spreading out a puddle. I can't believe this. They are patting. I am gulping. My eyes are leaking. Every other minute I get a hit on a flask. We've all punched hands. The fat one is Charles. The thin one's his brother, Neville. Here's me (repeating), 'Boys, this is embarrassing . . .' Here's Charles. 'Nough Joey. It was down to us, Joey, down to us. We feel right bastards 'lieve me.' A big shudder in my chest. Here's Neville, 'Man's best friend a dog is. Never lets you down, not never. Remember Redwing Charles? Bloody. Bloody lovely dog. When he got run over our dad he got upset, got a bit teary didn't he . . .' 'Yeah,' Charles goes, 'and you, you bawled your eyes out. And there was that baby Jack Russell, and our Gary's Alsatian and that boxer with the Boxer. He'd die for his dog, he said and his dog would die for him . . . Plenty men go for dogs, our dad, his dog, what and Elvis and Shep . . .' Here's me, I goes, 'I'm not . . . it's not about *a dog*. I told you, it wasn't my dog.' I goes, 'I don't want to talk about it. You wouldn't understand.' Here's us smoking on the bench. Here's Neville twitching like a vein. 'It'll be about a lady,' he goes, 'a love job!'

I don't need no persuading. I need more drink. They say they'll treat me to this club their mum runs where they've got an elasticated tab. I say yes. I need more drink. A motor coughs at the end of the path. Here's us walking to it. Neville drips Muttley over his arm. He's stroking her head, shaking his. Here's Neville: 'When our dad brought Redwing home she was horrible, all mashed, lovely dog, lovely. When I think about her you know I go, I go all really funny, inside.' Then he goes, in a whisper, 'Joey, I ain't never told anyone this, but sometimes I go hard, you know, . . . *outside*.' Here's me, I go, 'Oh.'

The motor coughs in a throat of purple trees. Cardboard L-plates. The windows and windscreen are creamed with flies. On the back window someone has written OH KILL ME in grime. Here's me: *This*, I think, this is one A-class day. I have a piss on a tree. My piss is green and reeks of, what is it? avocados we had yesterday . . . starters, some kind of dip. Charles stands next to me and has his. Here's him, in a whisper, over the streaming, he goes, 'I ain't never told anyone this, Joey, but if it helps I've been there. My first and only love was Mara. She played the sax in my mum's club oh years . . .' His voice goes faraway, 'Her lips. Her bottom lip was like arm muscle. What a kisser that woman, I still . . .' Here's Neville, he goes, 'What? what?' We're zipping up. Charles goes, 'Oh shu' up, Neville.'

We climb in. Charles drives, in fits. Inside we're smoking and sipping. My insides have melted, my headache is lifting. Outside, it's one long lemon-lit, blunted-building blur. Here's me, I'm wiping my nose on the sleeve of my tux. Then I'm holding my nose as Muttley is strapped up stiff, already reeking in the wonky heating; dead hot dog. What am I going to say to Steve? I can't tell Steve. Oh Christ, Steve loves that dog. What am I going . . . ? Here's Charles. He goes, 'We're not really robbers. You was just a one off, in the tux an all, it was all too much.' Here's me, I goes, through my nose, 'This is, boys, strictly one-off attire. Rat-arsed at a wedding last night, best mate's. Really I'm a . . .' I stop. Then I look at their necks. Here's me, I was going to say, really I'm a musician, like I've gone for years 'The Three Leaves' me, Steve, Eve, then 'The Two Leaves' me and Steve, now one me. I goes, 'I'm a postman.' It comes out weak. I'm thinking about it for miles. Postman. Postman Pat. I think, that's what I am. It's not just me day job, it's me. I feel whacked. Here's Charles, he goes, 'When I say we're not really robbers it's not really the honest God's . . . cos we are really robbers but we're not . . .' Here's Neville, passing the flask. '. . . very good at it yet. It was my fault, I brung him down. We had a house an all, nice little bizz, nice little bizz, double glazing, complete window outfitters, but I got a prob: dogs, debts . . .' Here's Charles, turning round to make sure I know that is one understatement. 'Under-state-ment . . .' He goes, 'Dogs. He's dog mad.' He puts his thumb on the horn and underlines it, 'Dog dog *mad*.' Here's Neville, 'Look out!' We crash.

Write-off. The motor is totalled; the bonnet is halfway crumpled up a brick wall. What a miracle escape. It's sort of stunning. Here's us sitting in there stunned. Here's us tumbling out. Here's them kicking the wheels. Here's me, grinning, feeling oh . . . Being nearly dead has pulled me right back up. Through the creamy glass Muttley's front paws are stuck straight up like she gives up. Here's me pointing in, going yap yap.

And I'm up all the way to the club.

'Our Club', their mum's place, lies below sea level, down stone stairs. Inside it's chrome, pink, gold, a round bar. Behind the bar a frosted hairstyle shakes cocktails up and down. Neville nods the word 'Mum' at me. I nod back; don't know why. There's so many women encrusted round the bar, on stools, all sorts, sipping. Shaking, sipping and kind of sad. Here's me, perked. I suddenly feel well handsome. '*Hallo* girls . . .' Here's Charles, Neville: '*Sssh!*' Neville stabs at a sign in pink ink: DRINKING ONLY. ABSOLUTELY NO CHAT FOR FIVE HUNDRED YARDS.

Here's us at a round wet table, drinking solidly, solemnly, at length. Lemon stuff, red stuff, green, purple stuff, sucking off the fruit. Here's me, I'm thinking loquacious. I'm thinking about the whole of my stinking life. I've never had a think like it.

Here's us, we're adrift, passing the five-hundred-yard mark, prising apart pistachio nuts, whispering over a huge, slushy cocktail, three straws. Their faces are pinky and sloppy with drink. We're just inches apart. Hundreds of miles away the bar is shimmering, glasses . . . women. I say, 'Eve walked right past me . . . didn't even recognize me . . . it was like a shock.' Here's Neville: 'The love job?' I nod. Then I can't stop nodding. Charles puckers up his lips and blows a red rubber kiss towards the bar. He's saying something but I can't hear. 'Here's me,' I goes, 'outside the church yesterday, being *the* Best Man, when this black Merc draws up and this glass-nylon leg gets out . . .' Charles, he goes, 'Mara, her underwear . . . sweet, Jee . . .' I goes, 'It was my ex-wife Eve.

7

I hadn't thought about her in five years but I always thought she was always thinking about me.' Neville goes, 'Go on go on.' I goes, 'I just thought someone was watching for me and they weren't. I just thought I had someone but I got no one, nothing.' '*Us*,' Neville sobs, 'you got us Joey mate, 'now on. Drink.'

He puts a straw in my mouth. And, before I know it's happened, it's happened again. Here's me sipping here crying. Here's Charles: 'Ma Ma Ma Ma-ra,' his red rubber kiss pings across the bar. Here's Neville: 'Redwing . . .' clicking his fingers low on the floor, 'Redwing, here . . . here girl.' Here's us, we're sipping here, crying.

Heavy Petting

I come from a long line of pet deaths. Bunny and Clyde . . .
Tiny and Twinkle. Sid and Nancy. Mungo . . .

But it's Godfrey who haunts me.

At night, when the cistern gurgles, it's like he's back with
a splash.

Majella hooped him at a fairground and brought him
home, dangling from her thumb, gulping mist in a plastic
bag. He wasn't expected to live for long. She plopped him
in the dead terrapin's tank: watched him loop. Blessed his
tank: named him after her ex-fiancé, the paratrooper, the one
who'd chucked her out on the street, howling. Godfrey.

Godfrey was like Godfrey: he was quick, ginger, flash, but
he was never mean.

He was so *bright* in our dingy house. He blew air kisses all
day, puffed out silvery smoke rings . . . link chains. A stray
sunbeam hit his glossy water and he sparkled. Round and
round: an endless U-ey . . . At first, Majella blew him kisses
back, showered him with presents from the pet shop: bright

coral-gravels, a pagoda, a stone-coloured hide'n'seek boot, a fluorescent pink plastic hanging garden . . . and sieved him out, with the tea-strainer, for long transatlantic journeys in the bath – and then she *turned*. She turned to clubbing, drugging, and a bloke called either Mr Ecstasy or Marv. Or both. Majella, my sister, went *rave* mad.

One day Majella was a laughter-line in a nightie, spitting on an iron, singeing a pleat down her navy work skirt; and next, she was this gum-snapping *stranger* pacing up our hall: wearing tight T-shirts with daisies on them, calling cabs at midnight; hipped out, with her belly button sticking out of flab. (Later, she had it pierced: it went septic. Septicaemia . . . She got gangrene. She had to go to hospital. It went the size of a yeasty currant bun. But that was *much* later.)

Majella really *loved* Godfrey but, after she hit the clubbing scene, got, as she called it, 'loved up', she hated him.

Listening outside her door I heard her chant above her telly, 'Ignore me now army boy. You *bastard*. You *bastard*, Godfrey. What are you? *You bastard*, Godfrey . . .'

I didn't think pretty Godfrey could live for long.

+

I was studying for A levels at the time, training hard as a Young Novelist, honing my powers of observation in little red notepads. (When I got my grades, the predicted A, A, A, I'd get to university five hundred miles away: leave home without one look back. I had to stay focused, unattached.) But I couldn't resist saving Godfrey. One wriggle in his tank, and I was hooked!

'Mum?' I said. '*Look!*' I'd airlifted him out from the hell-hole of Majella's bedroom: blown away his sky of talcum powder, reeled out a foot of Majella's tan-coloured, scummy tights, and set him down by the scummy cooker in the kitchen. Though he was thin – a red bone in a white sock – he was, I thought, *all the light in our house boiled down.*

In the hot kitchen Godfrey blinked his gold. 'Look Mum,' I said, 'isn't he *sweeeet?*'

Mum looked down: her cheeks steamed, flushed like two rubbed spots. Her eyes, under her sweaty eyebrows, gleamed. I looked from her to the brown sudsy cooking pots, back to Godfrey, back to Mum.

I thought: Poor Godfrey, he won't last for long. Out of the fire, into the pan.

+

Mum had gone . . . funny in the head. That's what Majella yelled, tapping her temple: 'You're *funny-in-the-head,*' as though Mum's head had been stacked (when we weren't looking) with comic books, sitcoms . . . I couldn't think of a better explanation myself. As I noted, in my novel-training notepads, when Mum *went funny* she went like Majella: *like that!* One day the air was a soft brown wall of unflushed loos, rusting geraniums, takeaway foods. Dust snuffed from the carpets thick as bonemeal. All day Mum made secret-recipe soups: threw great slop waves across the lawns. She'd scour the cupboards for odd ingredients. In went Majella's old school tie, an aubergine, one cake of Cherry shoe polish . . . Out puffed rust and rubble, smells that made the plants cave in.

Outside, our other pets howled on the lawns, sang like exiles, made a heady high white noise, scribbled their nibbled light pink legs in the sheds, kicked up for dinner time. The toy poodles shook their pale dreadlocks. Our albino rabbits stretched their dirty jaws. Across the neighbourhood, strays joined in: cats caterwauled. Mum stirred away in the kitchen. She boomed a silent radar: her animal attraction. The pets on the lawns crackled, eared up and somersaulted back. Or they'd bounce and pose above the grassy gore, suspended for a moment, hunched like fridge magnets.

In his tank Godfrey (plumped up), beaming bright, would pause. He'd leap above the pagoda, hang out in the hanging garden. Dirty strobe light smacked his back. His tail thumped. He swam on.

We had to ring for takeaways. At night, when the cat songs got too much, I'd lob our leftover cartons of chicken tikka, the chewy rinds from our takeaway pizzas, salty chip rejects, up out and into the long splattered grass. Shrieks? A scrummage. A feral pet race. The air filled with clods of earth: back-kicked peas. Tree-high stalks shook. As I noted in my red notepads, only the *very* fast survived.

+

Doctor Trang upped Mum's medication. The side effects, he said (zombie-ism, intense communion with small dumb animals), were a small price to pay, believe him. I did. I'd already noted the symptom: synchronicity. In the hot kitchen, when Mum paused, holding a ladle, Godfrey paused too; when one stirred, the other whizzed rapidly round.

In the kitchen Godfrey's light drew me to him. He surfed the surface; flayed gold . . . green . . . red. His tank bubbled like a miniature jacuzzi: full of air and spinning fat globes. He'd flip on his side, fin a zippy sidestroke, blow a little link kiss at Mum as she sipped, with deep concentration, at her wooden spoon. Mum looked down at Godfrey and blew him crumbs, a grape, a rubber fish face. They were one.

At least I knew, with Mum around, Godfrey was safe.

At night, dust snowed around me. My plimsolls squeaked on the sticky lino. Never mind, I told myself, opening my revision notes, I'll be up in Loughborough soon . . . maybe Edinburgh. Wales. The University of Ulster? Miles and miles away . . . Somewhere clean. I vowed then, catching glitter scales from Godfrey, a tinkle tune from deep down in the blue pagoda, when eventually I escaped, Godfrey was coming with me too. 'Godfrey,' I urged, '*stay* strong.'

'Manchester,' I whispered. 'Newcastle. Durham . . . You, Godfrey, and me.'

At night, our other pets sat in line on the black grass: ruby-red-eyed. They were the lifers: all born to us, given to us, at a time when we must have seemed, no, we were *exactly* like a photograph happily framed: there was Mum in rose-tinted C&A blouse; Dad, roastily tanned in his crisp blue cotton overalls. Majella and me in our steam-ironed bottle-green school uniforms (Majella's big hands on my little shoulders), showing our heavy-metal orthodontistry. Behind us surged a thunderous studio sky. Around us hopped the albino rabbits, the tortoise. The mongrels. The cats. Poodles . . . They all began to die.

Majella started clubbing it once a week, then twice . . . thrice . . . Mr Marv was a light voice on the line (a 'Yeah', a 'She in?'). He was a slice of shadow, a stripe of Adidas in the crack of a cab. Majella came home shiny, she sniffed, snapped her chewing gum at Godfrey. (Her luminous inks flowered first in the choke of the hall.) In the kitchen she drank tap water, spat green tubes of it through gaps in her teeth at me, at my homework; stared in at Godfrey as he flashed to and fro in his tank. Her face greyed, grew stone. She hovered over his tank, dribbled strands of her long beige hair in, eyes set wide apart: black-pooled, scary, like a shark's. Godfrey cowered in his hide'n'seek boot. I cowered too. 'Godfrey,' Majella chanted, 'I'm going to *get* you. What am I going to do, Godfrey? *Get* you.'

I didn't think Godfrey could survive for long.

Mum filled up pots, slopped the rejects out in long brown rattling arcs. Soup skin wobbled on the grass, shone like satin wheels. Pets raced from the sheds, squacked.

In the kitchen her pots heaved. A carrot went in. A bicycle pump, a jagged tin . . . Mum had the radio tuned to LBC. Godfrey swam rapids in his tank. His jowls flopped. His movements grew fevered. His tail rudder really whipped froth along. His little face, pressing flat for a moment against the glass, began to look quite – sad. Perhaps it was Majella? Ceaseless LBC? A tiny slit in Mum's synchronicity? Flitting across his features I'd see the face mask of an ex-pet: one of the terrapins: Sandy? Andy? . . . One of those who'd dried. Outside on the lawns, all the pets cried.

+

In my trainee notepads, I noted, sipping a Lemsip, 'We're all on medication now.' Mum had little white pills. Majella had her little white pills. Even Dad, who I was in love with, took massive painkillers. He had migraine. He'd come home from the railways like a train. Light stabbed him. Coffee killed him. Pineapple juice made him cry. He had migraine so bad he had to inject himself in the bathroom, using his leather belt as a tourniquet. (His injection kit was a toy briefcase, deadly black; inside, chrome cylinders, needles so thick they made your skin lock.) He had blinders. He'd charge home honking noise, smoking rust, with one eye spinning like a shot blue marble, the other scrunching up his forehead, his bobble hat thick with dust. I don't think he noticed the litter under his boots, or chicken tikka again for tea. I stood in the kitchen sipping blackcurrant Lemsip, studying my books, peeping in at Godfrey as he swam round . . . round.

Godfrey swam. He swam in brackish oily water and then, it seemed, he was deep in soup. He paddled past florets of cauliflower, dived under broccoli bombs, breasted logs of carrots, stinking shreds of chicken and lamb. He moved not in water but in stuff he really had to fin through. Gazpacho.

The air flowed with stock. Godfrey gave little shivery, fastidious leaps. Mum, stirring, leaped too. Leaning, trying to talk sense into Mum, one day, yelling above the radio blah-blah of LBC, I saw Godfrey take a leap at the edge. But the walls of the terrapin tank were too high. He leapt but a stray *calamaro* ringed his neck, winched it back, cut his arrow-like route to the floor. My heart flipped. Godfrey's battered, swollen, mottled, white-veined mouth glugged each time, sank to blank – down amongst the greasy olives, baggy purple prunes, hairy anchovies swishing by like unshaved legs: the assorted mucus beneath the murk. I'd mumble above his surface: 'Leeds . . . Aberystwyth . . . Godfrey, you hang on.' I changed Godfrey's water but Mum souped it straight back up. I tried putting Godfrey in my bedroom near my computer and neat stacks of homework but Mum kept bringing him down, sloshing, bashing his delicate lips brown. I tried to keep Godfrey on the up.

But I failed. I failed my mocks. An (un-predicted) D, D, E. When I told Godfrey he flickered away. I looked for him in the grey TV screen of his tank. 'I'm sorry, Godfrey,' I said. I turned to Mum. She stirred away.

I tried to stay focused, stay head-down, but . . .

I thought Majella was now heavily into the drug scene, was like a suburban drug queen, and I was worried. In the high streets, on Saturdays, she walked like a celebrity, in dark glasses, like *Ms* Ecstasy, grinding from the hip. Cruddy people tried to talk to her. Hordes of dirty, whey-faced kids whispered around her, begging for crumbs, for 'disco biscuits'. Majella brushed them off, and with a swing of her shiny nylon ginger hairpiece, a flick of her reddening belly button, she mooched away. She had loads of money. Notes fell around her, folded up, tiny.

I saw adverts in the papers for people to appear and confess personal family information on *Esther* or on *Vanessa*, and I was thinking of appearing. I'd snitch Majella up for her own good. I'd get her into rehab. Write to her from my tidy room. I circled the adverts with red biro and left them on Majella's littered grey bed, as a warning, a hint for her to *pull herself together*. I tapped Mum's arm in the kitchen. 'Mum?' Godfrey paused. 'Godfrey?' I said. 'Newcastle Polytechnic? Brighton FE?' Godfrey swam away.

+

Majella started clubbing it four times a week, five. She'd come home at around four o'clock in the morning, with Mr Marv. (She'd sleep maybe two hours, then speed off to work. Her eyes were like slots.) I'd wait up, reassuring Godfrey there'd be no game-playing tonight whatsoever, watching as his sides bulged at the scrape of a key . . . Mr Marv swung in first: smirked, picked up a dirty fork, toyed with its crusty prong, slid it up his sleeve. Majella doubled behind him: they were thin, shiny, daisy-topped. They'd sloppy-kiss, edge to the tank; rub each other up, but I was on guard, stayed solid, watched for the sudden lunge, the stabbing fork. They'd kiss out. Then, without warning, double back, *crash* into the kitchen tooled up to play, in between licks and despite my protestations, the Get Godfrey Game. They forked but Godfrey dived under the blue pagoda. They stabbed but Godfrey ducked into the hide'n'seek boot. He whizzed rapidly around a roast spud. Watching his dive I *felt* the full surge of his life force: he'd leapt back from a death wish; got firmly back *into* the swim; he swam away. Majella and Marv forked up sodden Coco-Pops, fried clumps of wire wool, crumbless stiff blue fingers of fish. Godfrey lived to flicker away.

+

Godfrey survived all through Majella's Marv stage, her Darren & speed stage, her LSD plus E stage. His stroke became really butch, determined. His nose grew blunt from speeding U-ies against the glass. Majella went clubbing six times a week. She looked thin-skinned. I could see the blood network through her face. She'd come home haggard in her Nat West uniform looking forty years old and emerge from her room, hours later, remarkably refreshed; showing tight arse-cleavage, her cheeks sparkly like two just-peeled spuds, her hair with a wide road of centre-parting, looking *just* eleven years old. In a rare burst of sisterhood, once, she showed me the three moves I'd need should I ever give up being a 'snitchy-bitch' and take up clubbing instead:

1. You put your fingers in the air and stab as though you're telling someone to piss off a lot.
2. You dance like snakes would.
3. You maintain an ironic hipster pose at all times.

But the music didn't really make sense to me: it seemed to consist of just the *one* sustained note and then random others! I couldn't see the point in all the drug-taking. I preferred, as a student Novelist, the occasional Lemsip, a paracetamol for my increasingly tense and nervous headaches, and life in the raw.

+

Our other pets went funny, *funnier*, in the head: showed acute symptoms of distress, neurosi, when they heard the squeal of a taxi. They bounced up and down on the grass, paced two steps forward, two steps back.

At night, sitting up with my computer, I'd hear Majella come home with a club drone, a Clive, a Tyrone, a Jeff . . . and I'd wait for the screaming to start. A yapping; barking. Squeaking. Flash of a penknife. Then, the rabbits would start. Carnage. Lights snapping on and off in the neighbour-hood; the grass electrified . . . shapes darting in and out of the sheds. One night I saw Mr Marv, Clive and Majella wipe blood from their mouths, a bit of white fur, a ridged bone, streaking through the grass, and I fell back on my bed and thought: I've got to leave this family *now*. I had to keep racing down to protect Godfrey from the Get Godfrey Games. In the kitchen Majella stabbed at his tank, screamed out her old howling rage, stabbed, as though Godfrey really was her *ex*-Godfrey, the keen-eyed paratrooper; as though she really expected a thick hairy wrist, a fist of fat freckled fingers, to spring from the tank: *Attack!* Godfrey ducked and dived, slithered and writhed: survived. On bad nights Mum had to run down in her nightie to quieten the dawn chorus squacking up the pear trees, squalling from the sheds. She'd raise her long arms and shush the insects lying crippled and crying on the broken but still-swinging greasy black grass. The cats and dogs, the rabbits and shieldless peeled tortoi staggered up the bloody garden paths to have their wounds licked.

Summer was awful. I failed my A Levels and then I failed my resits (Fs). Tiny died in the sheds (she was all loose inside, really awful, like a bag of curds), and then Twinkle got run over. The tortoi fell into a coma and died. Suzi developed some kind of tumour on her neck and started going for Dad as he stepped in through the door from work. Really for *his* neck. Like *flying* through the air, like hiding under the stairs or crouched in the airing cupboard like Patience on a stack of dank sheets . . . The vet said a tumour removal operation would cost about forty pounds. One day I came in from signing on and Suzi wasn't there. Dad said she'd gone: 'Doggone.' He'd probably let her loose on the motorway, the bastard.

So we only had Godfrey left. And Godfrey was getting bigger.

He lived on juicy blue flies that fell from the ceiling and cod in butter sauce. He really liked chips. If you plopped a chip in the tank Godfrey gobbled it down in one, like a piranha. Godfrey was so fat now he could barely turn around in his tank. He swam on though. He only paused in his heavy front crawl to listen to Mum's long radio monologues or watch her manic hands chop the air. He still blew her kiss and kiss kiss. Mum gleamed. She poured old cups of sugary sun-warmed tea on his back to keep his water level up; pulled a few rubbery fish faces; flipped in chips. With each look-in Godfrey swam with extra verve; blew out kiss and . . . kiss and . . . kiss. Sometimes, Mum kissed back. As the kitchen boiled up, Godfrey's tank became just like another steaming bowl of soup: he smelt, sometimes, really tasty.

I wasn't so happy then. I tried to keep my spirits up by writing an epic novel slowly by computer in the morning and swimming slowly in the swimming pool down the road in the afternoon. I was quite good at breast stroke and, as I breasted the clear blue water, I thought about Godfrey: his immense powers of endurance, his selflessness. I admired the sheer *purity* of his direction. His staying power. I would, I told myself, now eschew all Lemsips and paracetamol. I would be as Godfrey, and simply *endure*.

Dad started coming home late, becalmed, with rust marks like vicious love bites on his neck. I noted his clothes no longer billowed their usual bluey-grey cloud of concrete dust. Had he shaken it elsewhere? I thought: Yes. (I imagined a bottle-blonde in a nylon cream cardigan donned like a cloak . . . I drew a picture of her in my notebook, stabbed big juicy blackheads into her chin.) His boots also had new bootlaces on them. I swam and listed clues like that. I was even more worried about Majella. I could *smell* her rotting flesh. It smelt light green. I'd be up guarding Godfrey, watching late-night Hindu films on the telly, waiting for dawn to crack light across the old chicken tikka cartons on the still black lawns: I'd wait for Majella to come home. Majella staggered from her cab. I'd smell her first: rot. She'd come up daisies in the hall, push straight through me, sneer, throw the drug literature I'd got from Dr Trang back in my face, push me off. Her forehead and temples were glossed with sweat; above her hipsters the belly button rose from its punctured hood like a lump of red, still-cooking, bread. 'Majella?' I called. I had Dettol on hand, TCP ready. Majella staggered past me, zigzagged up the stairs, shook the light fittings, and slammed a heavy screen of dust from her door frame.

Godfrey swam in his tank. Gulped, slowly, round.

Mum's medications went haywire. She was talking more or less out loud: answering all the voices chanting inside her head. Under Dr Trang's direction she had to swallow his pills and lift her flabby grey tongue for his inspection. Mum swallowed. The muscles in her throat rippled. Dr Trang shook his head, perplexed, and wrinkled his nose.

Mum talked back to LBC on the radio, nodded vigorously at whichever other airwave was tuning her in . . . fuzzing her out. A new pet fan squeaked from the bread bin: a pet mouse. The mouse begged at her heels as she stirred the soup. Or it climbed on to the beige stubble plains of her worn-out carpet slippers, shiny pink mouse marigolds signing up supplications; squeak plaintive. Mum stirred the soup. The mouse scampered up her leg, her sleeve, her muscled arm, on to her shoulder, turned somersaults, squivelled hips, squeaked for attention, its cute black persistent eyes gleaming. Mum stirred on. The mouse cut a squeak through her airways. Godfrey, in his tank, splished up distraction: wacked up prawns, corn on the cob . . . splashed. The mouse tricked on. Wandering into the kitchen one hot afternoon, chewing my hand, I heard a – different squeak. Human: 'A carrot IS essential, mango chut—' The mouse was poised up on Mum's thumb, paws in beg mode, raised so its whiskers could tickle her own. Mum was squeaking, in a squeaky Nice-Aunty voice, the secret of her secret-recipe soups. She roared: 'Vanilla essence obviously, stupid mouse, ha ha ha fluff! One cornflake, leather thong . . .'

Godfrey broke surface. Red-eyed. Slowly dived. He no longer got a look-in.

Mum petted the mouse. She bound it to her gold wedding band, confided sauce notes at its peaked and quivery carpet-felt ears; *wheeed* it through a PEAK–trough–PEAK rollercoaster ride of brown kitchen soup air: all day. Or, with no warning, she leapt decibels: SHRIEKED! Godfrey swam on ignored, like me, up and down. Up and slowly, solidly down.

+

By day, stinking of chlorine, I wrote out job applications and listed my Reasons for Application. Sometimes I sat in my old dark-green school uniform adding a new chapter to my opus: Chapter 67 . . . Chapter 110. Or I'd look through my thumbed, smudged A Level textbooks and wonder how and exactly *at which point* I failed. At night I stared into Godfrey's tank and synchronized with his one thought: Swim *on*. Just *swim* on. *Swim* swim swim.

Then one day I came home from a dole recall interview, chewing my lip. I thought I'd just look in on old Godfrey and start a really pure and positive Zen afternoon: Go on. Just *get on*. Chapter 200. Chapter 201 . . . I caught Mum leaning over Godfrey's tank. She was sly-faced, hugely pored. Her mouse-fan was boxing with excitement, shrieking squeaks from the bowl of her collarbone; it leapt at her stiff ponytailed head, climbed her ponytail scaffold. Wheeeeed round. The mouse grinned as Mum, gum-frilled, tippled and dribbled the contents out of her brown pill bag.

The little white pills slid on a slide through Godfrey's murk, became, I noted, with their powdery star tails, like ultra-white planets in flux. I saw Godfrey, buoyed up by half a cheese'n'viscous roll, by a boiled egg, pickled and embryonic like new baby skin – pause. The planets glazed his right side-eye, shock-waved, rearranged. You . . . *good* Godfrey, I urged, Ignore. Just swim *on* . . . Godfrey. You *swim* on! Godfrey swam on, swam and swam on till, with a flash of tail rudder, a shiver, a final soup-thwacking U-ey, he – gulped. His throat rippled and he gulped again.

I went into the garden and, lying out among the stale pizza crusts, with big raindrops splashing on my forehead, I began to cry.

Godfrey lay at the bottom of the tank, slowly burbling, like a miniature ginger whale.

+

Doctor Trang gave me pills. I had growing pains, he said. He patted my hand kindly and suggested I wash more. I smelt a bit fishy. I was a pretty little thing underneath all those eyebrows. I wandered the high streets, up and down, as the drugs made me march, and thought about a new novel I would write by hand, using pencil. No more computers. I'd get back into the raw.

In the kitchen, Mum shouted at the mouse-fan and the mouse-fan ran to fetch a friend. The two mice looked up and nervously conferred as Mum ranted and confused them, sent a pea-green football flying off her wooden spoon. They chased.

I bent my knees to the tank and looked, with my slow-motion blink rate, into the thunderous grey matter where something large and orange glowed. 'I forgive you, Godfrey,' I said, reaching for a fork. 'I'm . . .' I stabbed, stammering, 'o-out of it ta-*too*.' I smelt light green: saw, on my periphery, luminous daisies bloom. 'Godfrey,' I said, 'the ga-game is o-o-ver.' Godfrey bellied up. Beside me, I heard Majella sob.

After a Dance

Once he knew she'd do it, he put his foot down and drove his father's car through narrow roads, fielded on each side. She saw the house by a long green sweep of the headlands.

He parked between a tractor and an ancient box-shaped car. As he turned the headlamps off she caught a gleam of chrome and of dark leather seats. Birds flapped from the windows of the car. Hens. Her mouth opened to cry – the whiskey she'd drunk fumed in her throat.

She would recall that night often.

The house was dark, it had long passed midnight, yet the boy made no effort to be quiet. It seemed to her he made a great deal of noise – banging the car door, jangling the coins in his pockets – as though to advertise their presence. He had told her, whispered in her ear, the house was his Uncle's but he had the run of it; he was the favourite Nephew. When the Uncle died the house would be his and the Uncle was very old now and frail. He walked across the yard and into a thicker fold of black; the tips of his boots scraped stone.

She could just see the white in his shirt. All the old ones had been dying lately, he said; sometimes it happened like that. He returned with a large ornate key which he held up in front of her face. She smelt soil, rust.

It occurred to her to be frightened of the boy and of the dark house and of the man inside. She would not know her way back to the holiday home, she had paid no attention at all to the route. She shivered, rubbing at her bare upper arms. When he took her hand she allowed herself to be led under the low hood of the porch but she did not return his pressure. The key rattled in the lock. Then, she felt him bend towards her. The dark concealed his expression but she smelt the drink-clouds on his breath and her heartbeat altered, he was so still. It seemed he might . . . His arm was along her waist. He was humming. Mock-solemnly, he kissed her hands. She was back in the centre of the yard. The boy hummed a tune the band had played in the dance hall and swung her round so the skirt of her dress lifted up above her knees and floated in their breeze. He breathed into her hair, clucking like a hen, his breath and hands very warm, till she laughed and became easy with him again.

The door opened into a kitchen lit by the faint red lamp of the Sacred Heart and the remains of a fire burning down into a grate. A dog stretched ragged, pink-tinged limbs for a moment but did not rise. She watched as the boy blessed himself rapidly at the font. Then, smiling, she blessed herself too. The water from the font dripped from her forehead on to her dress. The boy led her through the tall kitchen furniture, and, holding hands, they tiptoed up the stairs.

Halfway up the house, behind a thickly painted door, a man snored loudly – climbing and descending scales. She heard the sound of a body turning over heavily on springs. And it did not seem to her to be the frail turn of an old man. The boy tugged on her hand. When she did not move he began to whisper in her ear. Then she felt his mouth on her, large and wet. She felt his stubble burn on her chin as he half lifted her up the next stair. They continued up through the house. She heard behind them, the Uncle's deep ascending snore.

The room had belonged to his Maiden Aunts. He let her in first, pinching her as she passed.

She said she could smell old ladies: damp, lemon and mothball, a faint tang of disinfectant. She said, wasn't it terrible to end up all smelling the same? He patted the wall for the light switch. The light – a low, bare bulb – blinked twice, then, it seemed to her, swung into light. It lit the dead centre of the room. Thick yellow dust drew back across the floor. The room was barely furnished: two stripped, single beds, two tall glass book cabinets, a square iron chest. Two armchairs sat in shadows along the wall. She asked about the Maiden Aunts. He said they'd died the year before. She said, walking in, pointing out tracks on the lino, wasn't it terrible to be old and make the same journey every day? She said she wasn't looking forward to it. She asked—He said it was a long story. He would tell her more about them in the morning. They could do all the talking in the morning. She had to be quiet now as the Uncle would hear. He patted a bed and sat down to unlace his boots. The bed let out a tiny hiss of air. He allowed the boots to drop heavily onto the floor. There were no sheets or pillowcases, he said, they'd have to make do.

Slowly, she began to undo the buttons on her dress. The boy walked over to the iron chest and pulled back the lid. Her fingers trembled on the buttonholes. She watched as he lifted out a blanket. When he came towards her she said, very quickly, pointing out stains on the mattress, your Uncle's generous with his room. Do you take all the girls here? He threw her a side of blanket to tuck in but he did not smile. She pulled her dress up over her head. He was in the bed, watching her in her underwear. She tugged the ribbon out of her hair. Under the hard light she felt – exposed and would have turned it off but it seemed . . . after the way they'd been together in the car. A creak on the staircase decided it for her. She was in the bed with him. He was laughing at her: did she think it was his bad old Uncle . . . *listening*? Still smiling, he climbed on top of her. The bed creaked. It seemed to her it creaked out of time with their movements. It was not like the promise of it in the dance hall or in the car. In the car, it was warm from the heater and their quick breathing. The radio played green and yellow on their skin. He said—

She heard but she could not retain his words. He snapped something at her and then fell heavily on top of her, asleep. It was as though he'd struck her and then been struck unconscious himself. The whole of his weight pushed into her collarbone. One of his hands lay tangled in her hair. She lay under him, stunned. What was it that he'd said? She began to cry. She heaved him over and sat up and looked at the four corners of the room, the four, blurring, yellow mounds of dust, and back at the boy in the bed. Dust tumbled across the floor. And she was on the other bed, unable to suppress her noise and then unable to believe she was the one making the noise. Perhaps she had drunk more than she'd thought? When she raised her head, it was to the sounds of his whistling snores. Her eyes ached. Her hands and feet were frozen. Shivering, she went over to the chest. The blanket she pulled out was damp and so heavy, as though it could break her under its weight. She was lowering the lid of the chest down when she caught a flicker of green-white: a deep pile of linen sheets, pillowcases with lace edgings; her fingers felt along raised, embroidered writing. So, she was not good enough for sheets. She looked over at him, at the side of his long hair, the top of his shoulder, the spread of him under the rough blanket, and felt a spuming hatred. She slammed the lid of the chest down, but he did not wake.

She would recall that night often. What was it that he'd said? She did not sleep. She listened to the boy's snores and, from the room below, the snores of the Uncle. She tried to turn the light off but the connection with the switch had snapped. All night the light burned. At one time she stood up for a book from the glass cabinets but found them both locked. The small glass panes were smudged with fingerprints. At another time she stood at the window watching the light change the colour of his father's car, the rusty scales of the tractor, the glittering chrome and brass and mirrors of the Uncle's car, the road and hills outside and beyond them a line of mountains coming out of the mist. At last she heard doors opening and closing, the rattle of a tin bucket. A close morning cough. She saw two black hens race across the yard, a shine holding on to their backs. Dressed, she lay on the bed with her hands folded neatly on her lap, waiting for him to wake.

They sat at the breakfast table. He played with the dog, making it beg for scraps while the Uncle served a fry-up from the stove – eggs, bacon, black pudding – shuffling from the table to the stove in carpet slippers. The sound of them all eating. The Uncle asked was she enjoying her holiday and she said that she was.

At Least Pull Your Jumper Up

He put his key in the lock and the house turned. Clara announced she'd booked the town hall for the thirtieth of July and if he didn't want to marry her all he had to do was not turn up. He said, you can't do that. She said, well I have.

He said – he was a policeman – he used his policeman voice.

You need id and I have to be there in person.
    She said I had id. Your passport and your twin brother.

She wasn't kidding.
    She wanted him to commit.

She said, don't do the mute thing.

He said, I am committed. I'm committed to you. To this . . .
He gave her his four minute silence, working his jaw.
    She said. I can hear you. I know you're swearing. She

pushed her bushy hair (it seemed all one extremely thick strand) behind her ear. Here it came. You think I wanted to live here?

She'd wanted what he called, in his copper shorthand, the works. In no alphabetical order, k for kids, h for hens. G for general green stuff, C for the country. She'd got No and no. And yes to Legoland. They'd got a tall thin new-build. Open-plan. When the front door slammed you could feel it all the way through your hooves. I'm home. He only had a thirty minute commute. She had an hour and a half either way. He owed her. He said we're ok the way we are. She said, you think? Really?

In bed she pulled out a bridal magazine and began to under-line sections using a pink highlighter. Bouquets. Favours. Sash . . .

He laughed it off. It was just one of her ideas.

Clara often had ideas. The ideas would be in the air and then one would bolt for her head. They'd been together thir-teen years.

She sent out the invites, embossed.

He laughed it off. He said it's just one of Clara's—She'll never go through with it. His mates said, but seriously, Estonia or

Barcelona? He said, it's just . . . It's her sense of humour. They said, this is going to cost all of us, so stop messing about.

He said I don't want a stag night, all right?

Clara had a hen night, a week of facials and public vomiting in Paris, via Eurostar. She went dressed as a cat. She was, in fact, a little too stout to be a cat. He didn't hold back, he told her so as she was doing her whiskers, taking off one of her paws. She said your suit is hanging up in the wardrobe. I've had a word with Rob. He'll pick you up in the morning of the 31st.

He said, have I not made myself clear?

He said, Clara, you'll look a fool.

She brushed past him, crimping one side of her mouth down. You'll be there.

He boiled over when she left. A week on his own. The house was both noisy and quiet without her, like someone had put an echo CD on. His friends were on his stag do, subsidized by Clara. There goes the kitchen extension.

He said, this is all just some . . . Why?

She said, because. Because you owe me.

On the Monday he drank his way through a six-pack and ate from the microwave.

Tuesday, was a ditto. In fact ditto till Friday. Friday he decided to treat himself to a takeaway, not a curry or a Chinese. If she could spend their money, so could he. He flipped through the yellow pages and his thumb found DINNER FOR 1. Home cooked gourmet meals.

Fuck it, he thought, and he showered and changed into his wedding suit. Shiny shoes, no shirt, just his bear-like chest.

In here, he said, to the caterer, a tall pretty girl of forty-eight or so. He showed her the card table he'd set up in front of the TV. She laid out his dinner. She said, I could serve if you like, it's all in. He shrugged.

Just his loud chewing.

And *Taggart*.

She poured him a glass of wine, stood by with a plate of vegetables in a steaming bag.

She said, when he looked at her, don't even ask. But I'll have a drink.

Her name was Tara. She had a Ph.D. in philosophy, something he knew two things about. He told her. He also knew a joke about a cat. He told her that too. She looked at him and laughed with her head right back, like her head was tilted and he saw all the way down the red pipe of her throat.

She had large hands and the same size feet as him. Are you . . . he said. She sighed before he could finish.

Yes, she was. She held out her hands. These, she said, used to drive a Humvee.

Her real name was Trent.

She had been, until recently, a paratrooper but was now in

process. She said, I'm half the woman I want to be. She said, I've got to stop using that line.

She told him about her operations in Thailand, how she was still in the process of changing her voice.

She talked on. She was living proof, she said, that you can make a silk purse. He didn't get that joke. He pulled out the whisky.

Later he said, I don't know what it is but I can really talk to you.

It's because I'm missing my quota of allure and mystique, Tara said. I'm getting that in an injection next week. You can still read me like a bloke.

She said, mate, I'm kidding.

There was a long silence while they drank. She could drink like ten men.

She did. He was all over the place, spinning at the centre of the room.

Tell us, Tara said, when the room stilled.

What?

You know what?

Jake gave her his deadeye but it didn't have its usual effect.

I don't want to, Jake said. Because he did have something he was saving up for his deathbed, before his final glottal stop. Something he'd been holding back from Clara. It was the thing, the thing he thought about when he wanted to stop her getting in. The dark one. The thing.

He mumbled something about his dad.

Oh fuck off, said Tara. That's so tired. You turn the TV on and someone has to tell about their dad abusing them or about something cruel they did to someone's cat. So what was it?

Jake looked at her like she'd robbed him.

Write it down then, Tara said.

I don't wanna . . . Jake said. All he wanted was to go out on the beat and find someone and just question them for hours. Stare at them over the counter, till their eyeballs bled and they'd sell their mothers. He got down his spare uniforms. OK, Tara said, kicking off her heels, but I get to drive, and the next six hours they were out in the cop car, blue light on, collecting DNA on the motorway, idling in a lay-by, full of twitch and pounce like a louse in a hairline.

Dawn rose like a length of streaky bacon. Which was when the horse appeared. No not a horse, something not fully grown. A white pony, greyish white, cantering up the wrong side of the motorway, passing the Fiats and the Peugeots and the long-hauls, stopping in front of their car, breathing into a bag of sparkling frost.

*

The mute thing.

Do you see that? Tara said. She put her hand on his arm, squeezed.

Tell.
    Jake shook his head.
    Write it on the windscreen then.
    And Jake did. The words, spelled out in black fly-gore, written under the eye of the horse, were Blind. Old. Lady.

And it was like the blind old lady left his head. Finally.
    He'd kept the blind old lady folded up and dirty inside his head, like a manky twisted and bloody nightie and whoosh she was gone disappearing into the back end of a pony, cantering away into pine forest and mist and he felt just lighter and better.

I do, Jake said, the next day. And he did. He would. He will, from now on, whatever the lady wants. Yes.
    Yes to anything highlighted in pink. Button holes. Favours. Yes to kids and anything beginning with c for commitment. H for Hens. And, after last night, and a crumpled fender, anything the future brings, even home security. Year of that then B for Belly, and too much beef, then club Bouncer. Yes to the portable future. Bye to holding hands with Tara-Trent in the revelatory dawn. K for the kiss best forgotten.

*

Clara, in a dress peaked and icy as egg whites, led up the aisle by his better bet, his reserve, his life-long spare, Rob, his twin brother, felt a tremor of grief pass up her arm.

Rob loves me, she thought, amazed but unsurprised.

At the altar, or what passed as an altar, a square of fake marble, complete with fake potted orchid, with, she saw like an omen, a fag end crushed in its soil, said after all, after thirteen years of consideration, and a bolt from the blue, with I love Rob too stamped through it like rock, she'd much rather not.

Harp

I didn't take his Reeboks, somebody else will get his Reeboks, it was the harp I was after, a *friggin* harp.

Let's say, it cost me something and it cost me nothing. It cost me me run round the Serpentine. I run round the Serpentine late afternoons, come rain, come shine. Got to get some cold air in, Underground out. You can die breathing this farty stink. I *know* people who've died breathing this. See those shapes in sleeping bags, in rags? They're not sleeping, no, they're dead. See, and it's my motto: you've got to keep fit if you live like shit.

I'm up to forty a day now, forty a friggin day.

How it was I was doing my system, finished up on the Northern line, and I was just about down, I was down. I was thinking maybe I'd worn it out, I had four pounds and fifty-five pence in brown. A year ago I averaged nine, ten a day. I had a system. You've got to have a system and then you got to work it. I worked the lines, one a day so Monday would be, say, the Circle, Tuesday Victoria, Wednesday Piccadilly . . .

and then every two weeks I juggled them for luck. You've got to shake yourself down, keep moving. What I did then was I sung solo, two songs. One song to stop them, the second to gather them in. Up and down the line. Just had to open my mouth and the money poured in. Except you get stale.

So I was down, let's say it was a combination of factors, and I had this bruise coming up from this bloke, didn't see it coming. Caledonian Road he comes up and took my chin, thought, leave it out, and moves my face from side to side, thought maybe I could get his pocket. Thought I'd seen that 'I Am An Artist' shit before. Gonna invite me to your studio are you? Gonna make me a star ya ya? Shit. Think I'm going to hang around in tan tights? Think I need a pimp to sing? Think I don't recognize one? But my timing was off and he cuffed me. Caught his rings on my ear. A while back and I'd have been quicker than his eye and off with his wallet and his watch like the wind. So I was holding my ear at King's Cross and I was thinking maybe I'd pick some scraps before my run and I was zipping down the escalator and I heard it and I thought, I've got concussion, that bastard's concussed me, but then I saw it and I said to myself, Hal-lo! it's an angel. It's an angel with my angle.

This fat boy was twanging a harp. He was pulling the strings out and just letting them go but even so it sounded fantastic and he'd got a hat with more takings in it than I'd had all day, a top hat, a *top hat*, and I started in with the elbows through the people and I saw stars and little birds twittering round my head and I thought *it* I am having. Having *it*.

He was dressed in gold, total. Gold jeans and a gold silk shirt, gold laces on his Reeboks. A gold watch he kept looking at. The stool he was sitting on, that was spray-painted tinsel gold. Beaming and glinting like a target.

'Hallo,' I said – I've got really good teeth, the front four are capped ultra-white, cost this bloke a fortune long time ago, so let's say I don't smile for nothing – 'I'd give you something but I've got no change. I'd give you something as that's really made my day that has, that a harp is it, baby one is it?'

What fatboy did was stretch and yawn and look bored, probably had a million and one morons all day going, 'Harp is it? Where d'you get it?' I've seen it. Probably thought slum it for the story, do it for a giggle. Seen those gimps in dinner jackets with their violins and their music stands, give me a break, and it was noisy as people were still throwing him change, and it wasn't even the friggin rush hour, *silver* change, and he pulled a couple of strings and let's say I was thinking, give the people a scale at least boy, and I matched them for notes. I just opened my throat, it's a gift I have, it's how I get by and I scat it. I decorated the harp with my notes. He said, listen to this, he said, 'Your voice been trained.' He was totally a-mazed. *Trained.* I said, *'Trained?* Friggin University of Life, mate.'

He was looking at me then, all Mr Marvel, and I saw it. I saw my dinner on a plate. Let's say he thought I'm a story. A story for his mates. Spread it on girl, *spread* it on thick.

I sang. I sent out some bell notes and we did a little duet, a little bit of blue with a harp. Fan-tastic. People threw us notes. I just needed a little time for my plan. How to get the harp? Let's say, I surprised myself a bit as my heart was banging like I'd done a run and my left armpit was dripping. I was breathing like I'm breathing through a rag. I was just about to mug and go but then he upped up and he'd got a rucksack and everything, the stool, the coins, the harp, folded up into this little rucksack. He strapped it on his back – shit! Double buckled so let's say, he wasn't as thick as he looked. And then I looked at his eyes – bing-go! – and I kept up this humming so I'd got his ear cocked and then I knew he was high as I timed his sniffs, that neat little rich-boy nose was going to go. *Sniffed it.* Hallelujah. A shrimp brain.

Turned out he goes to music college. *Music college.* Turned out he was 'bunking off'. I thought, he isn't lining it, he's shooting his nose, he's probably thinking she'll have something. All low life has something. I'll have that baby harp boy. That baby harp will be mine. Told him my name was Bebe, know what I mean, tell them what they like. Turns out his name is Martin. *Martin.* Give me a break.

I said, 'Well, Martin, that's a great name, make it up yourself?' Made him laugh, he'd laugh at shit. 'Well, Martin, I'm not kidding when I say you've really made my day, you've *made* my day. What I'm going to do is, I am going to buy you a beefy burger. I am going to buy you a burger with chips. I am going to buy you a beefy burger with chips, with a cup of tea and with – the story of my life.'

Whipped him out of the station and over the road and sat him down in the Wimpy like it's my kind of town. I said, 'I want the works, the *works* for this man.' I said, 'No thanks, Martin, I've got to watch my weight.' (No *way* I'm going to eat that moon cowshit, think I want a spongy brain, think *I* want a spongy brain?) I said, 'OK, for you, I'll have a cup of tea.' I dropped him some speed. My fingers were so fast. On form. Back on form and tabbed his chips. (I clocked the rucksack. He had it strung round his knee, twice.) I told him I love watching men eat. Martin loved that. Martin loved being called a man. Give me a . . .

And then he went all speedy. He looked at his watch like it was going to speak to him or decide to explode in his face. His hands drummed the table and slopped the tea and made the plastic ketchup bottles jump. He gabbled on with his mouth stuffed. I got my hand on his leg and rubbed. This is Martin's life story: Hendon. *Hendon* with his mum. And one helluva (Martin's words) one helluva coke problem, 'I just can't get enough of it,' (we laughed like hyenas). And guess, Martin plays in a band called Midas. 'That explains all the gold,' I said, slapping my forehead at cleverness. 'Right!' said Martin. (We laughed like hyenas.) 'Well, Martin,' I said, 'your life story has sorely moved me. I will now buy you a dessert. I will buy you an ice cream dessert. I will buy you a banana split with synthetic cream and chocolate juice and you want it with nuts?'

I said, 'Well Martin, you want a coke?' (Oh, how we laughed!) 'With a dollop of ice cream?' I had a hand on his knee and on the strap of the rucksack. I was fondling both. I said, 'Well, Martin, we come from different planets. My life is on the mean and narrow tubes, picking and a scrapping a livin' an trying to keep clean. You like this Country 'n' Western style?' I said, 'Martin, this is my life story.' Then I gave him my full Bebe Come Home. Got him all *stirred*. I told him in my normal talking tone.

He'd got ice cream and burger all over his chin. Let's say, I sorely reduced him with mad food and drugs. Let's say it was a combination of factors. I said, 'Yo, Martin, is that a Rolex?' and it's bing-go-city, sent him over the edge, *over the edge*. I said, 'Martin, I know we've only just met but sometimes a stranger . . .'

Turns out it belonged to Martin's dead dad, know what I mean? 'Martin,' I said, 'can I get you something? Chocolate fudge cake, maybe, a cappuccino? Milk is very good for you, it lines the stomach. A man like you needs a stomach-lining.'

Ever seen a face crumble? The nose was streaming, the eyes were streaming, the lips all helpless and the chin wiggled and wobbled, a volcano stirred full of snot, ready to explode under his face. I said, 'My Baby.' I rushed to him and put my hand on his hair and timed his convulsions. I kissed his forehead like a mummy. 'My Baby.' I said, 'Here let me get closer and get on your knee, here let me get that damn thing off you. Jeeze, it weighs a . . .' And then I was sprinting to the friggin door with the friggin rucksack. I had the friggin harp, the friggin harp I have got. Zoom zoom zoomed across the lights. Down the Underground.

Forty a day I'm up to now. Forty a day.

Plastered

My name's Tony Wornel, to cut a long story short. I believe in acting on first impressions, so when I see a bird at a party I go up to them, find their best feature and say, 'Great hair,' or, 'Hey,' pointing, '*cat's* eyes.' It works one time out of ten. That's not a bad average. When I say 'works' I mean social not sexual intercourse. I don't believe in using birds like that. I like a chat. I subscribe to a number of interesting magazines. I've got a stack of magazine knowledge inside me and, as I work in market research, I'm really good at moving the know-ledge round. After a good night out, if I've scored my one in ten, got a little *parlez-vous* going, when I get back home I feel really full of the possible. Even if it's been raining or even snowing, even if the backdrop is like depressing. I get back home and bound upstairs to my bed and think about what a *great* evening I've had.

Katy, to cut a long story short, really did have 'great hair'. It was up around her like a halo, almost like an Afro, but kind of wheat-coloured. It was her who started me off on my interior design. Like, time to sort out my spiritual home. Like I had to clear out, then decorate a really dark place. Like a cellar or a crypt.

My name, as I've said, is Tony Wornel, and I'm thirty-two years old and I've just left home. I mean my parents' home, Mr and Mrs Wornel. I still lived at home as it was cheap: I got my cleaning done, my clothes ironed and my food on time. Renting's a mug's game. I lived right up by Manor House station so it was straight down the Piccadilly Line in the mornings. No messing. My bedroom was more of a bachelor pad. Like a spread. Well, I could afford it. I had a mirror on the back of the door so I could see myself lying back on my big chrome bed. It's like all my exteriors were sorted: leather, pin lighting, black carpet, chrome. Built-in wardrobes so it was all strictly minimalist. Like I say, I'm good with information. I've got the top-quality range of electrical equipment and my own phone. If the phone rings I'm always playing jazz. Count Basie. You know, shit like that.

Renting really *is* a mug's game. This bedsit is now more of a lock-up: my gear's all squashed in and looks a bit stupid. Now I'm almost hoping, what with the mega insurance premiums, the whole lot gets nicked.

I could bring birds back home as well if I wanted.

My parents weren't bothered. They'd watch TV all night like switched-off robots with human eyes. They'd only switch on again if Helen – God Almighty – my twin sister rang up from Australia.

Me, I like to keep busy. I like to play hard. In the evenings, if I'm not out partying, then I'm reading through my mags, or playing my electric guitar or my jazz CDs. I've got a Complete Jazz Lover's Collection from the *Sunday Times Magazine* (though I'd say jazz is more a taste I'm acquiring). What I'd really like is to play in a rock band, as a hobby. Hence the electric guitar. I can strum it a bit but, really, I can't play it standing up yet, and rock bands won't exactly provide chairs. I've got to get that sorted. Gigs are great venues for chatting up birds. You can see all the good ones from the stage. The ones up for it, for a chat.

I meet a lot of birds at work with 'great eyes', 'clear hand-writing', 'nice handbags', but, because market research is such a cut-throat business, there's never any time for a good old chat. Since my accident though, they've been all over me like a rash. There's a gang at work known as the Marketeers, and they're really tight. They form an even tighter circle later on in the pub. At work, at Research Services Ltd, they don't notice the real me because of my persona. I'm like Squirrel Man, squirrelling away at my information. My job is to pump information into the computer *as* the gang are handing in their clipboards. It's pressurized stuff. Their job is quite pres-surized as well – what with having to stop tetchy people on the streets and at airports. It's one of those work hard, play hard places. I'm quick. I'm efficient. And people only notice if you make a mess. They don't know that old Tony Wornel becomes Tone the minute he gets back home and takes off his office jacket and puts on his leathers. They don't know that I sleep in black satin sheets and play electric guitar or that sometimes I lie back on my big chrome bed and feel really full of the possible.

The time I met Katy was quite a highlight and started me tripping into my interior, which, as I've said, is actually quite a dark place. Like I thought, It's about time I got that sorted. Like properly lit. As I said, I'm thirty-two years old. I like to play hard. I like to go on first impressions and go with the flow. I like to augment my magazine knowledge with personal experience. Some of my evenings out can be like adventures. To cut a long story short, the night of my accident was one such. I mean adventure. It was raining first off, which was annoying as I'd only Mum's poxy new polka-dot umbrella (which is shaped like a parasol and has the radius of a saucer and if my hair gets wet it goes fluffy and horrible, and also a bit bald-looking). I was in the Coach and Horses first for a few pints, peaked a bit too early, and then off I went to this party on the Amhurst Road. I just followed these three birds holding a couple of cans. In this party, though, it was like *all* black birds and me. They looked at me really funny and that might have been because I'm like white, and it might have been because I'm like a white bloke, and it might have been that I didn't actually bring any drink and was pretty tanked up already and still, unfortunately, holding the parasol umbrella. '*Great* party,' I said, just as the music went quiet.

I've read somewhere, in a magazine, that if friendliness fails (which it did), acting a bit berserk in a potentially dangerous situation can act as a protective shield. So I started dancing a bit, like Mary Poppins on E, thrashing around, and, when I came to, I was outside on the pavement, kind of down on my nose. For a long time. And I hurt all over. I felt a tug at my shoulder and a voice saying, 'Oh, leave him, Katy, he's drunk.' I rolled over, groaning. I looked up and I saw it. *Great* hair.

'My name,' I mouthed, 'is Tony Wornel.'

To cut a long story short, that's how I met Katy and Tracy: a sweet bird and a sour one. They took me back to their flat on the Amhurst Road. I was screaming, 'I'm *Tony Wornel*,' don't ask me why. The whole empty road was spinning like a spin-dryer. I had concussion. The parked cars and the shining brown pavement was sky one minute, and the stars were like under my feet making a horrible crunchy noise the next. Then the stars were exploding like fireworks. That was great. Katy and Tracy lived about five flights up, no lift, which wasn't so great. I had an arm round both of them. They had to practically carry me. This Katy one was really soothing. It turned out they're both like – *nurses*! ICN! My luck! When I come round I'm in Patient Heaven, feeling no pain, floating on a couch covered by scarfs and like girly junk (like pots of blue nail polish digging in my back), and these two nurses were like intensively caring for me, daubing me with red *essence de hospital*. It was like feminine and cosy in the flat. The whole place was asway with plant tendrils and smelt of pasta and like hot wine. The carpet had giant jigsaw puzzle outlines on it and a game of Monopoly full of housing estates. It looked lived in. And, though it was feminine, and I like, as

I've said, manly-minimalist, I felt right at home. Lying there, at the centre of it all, as it were, I get full of the possible. I thought, if *my* interior was a room, then this is the kind of room it should be. What a great evening! I get a revelation. I spend the whole night on the couch. I get to sleep with two birds. Tracy, the sour one, said she's not going to bed while 'he's here', so they both had to sit up all night nodding off in their armchairs like proper night nurses. I did directional moaning each time I saw Katy nod off in particular. She was great awake, really caring: doing the whole business: feeling my pulse, taking my temperature, the works. In the morning, my luck held out because, actually, I did have a cracked femur· and I had to go to hospital. It was really great all going to work, as it were, together.

To cut a long story short, the moment I got that plaster of Paris on my leg, well, it was brilliant. It was like all I'd needed was that extra bit of support. A prop. What a sea change at work! When the birds clocked me on my crutches limping along in this snowy white knee-length plaster, immediately they're all dead nice to me and want to write on my cast. They even make me a get well card. Get Well Tony Wornel, except they spell my name wrong. Thereafter, when I get to parties, instead of me having to do all the describing – 'Great hair', 'Lovely teeth', 'Coloured contact lenses, *surely?*' – birds more or less come up to·me. I guess it's because I look so vulnerable leaning forward on my crutches. Personal injury is a great conversational gambit. Even on the Piccadilly Line. Instead of me saying, I got the shit kicked out of me for gatecrashing this party, or like, These birds beat me up, I say, I did it skiing, or, There was a fire at home and I had to jump out of the first-floor window holding my baby brother. It's brilliant. I get to shift quite a lot of my magazine knowledge. I get just great social intercourse. And the backdrop, as it were, comes forward.

+

In the mornings the sun was really bright. The birds sang. I mean, instead of the usual dense racket, I was hearing tunes.

All the privet hedges shone and the tops of cars and even the puddles outside the station glinted kind of merrily. Midges danced about in the air. When I pulled my blinds up in the morning I felt like I was pulling up two extra eyelids.

Of course I went back to Katy and Tracy's flat a number of times to thank them for their many kindnesses. I got their phone number as well. The first time I brought nothing too fancy, something fairly understated: a bunch of blue cornflowers to match Katy's eyes and a box of after dinner (hint hint) mints. They couldn't let me in though, as they were just about to go on shift. The next time I got to sit on the couch, right at their centre, as it were, for a while, and just chat and chat away, and Tracy even went out and left me alone with Katy, who I much preferred of course anyway. Unfortunately, the phone rang about then and Katy had to rush back to hospital due to an emergency situation. Nurses *really* work hard.

At work, at Research Services Ltd, well, it was all great. Once a week I cleaned the graffiti off my plaster of Paris with

Tippex and shoe whitener so it was like brand new and just cried out to be scribbled on. Some of the birds were really extra-nice to me so there was plenty to think about when I got home and lay on my bed listening to my jazz CDs. When my leg plaster was clean it became like the Office Notice Board. Birds wrote things like: GARY KIBLIN IS A TWIT. Gary would come along, kind of sarcastically, in his big black baggy suit, and cross out the t. Quite a crowd gathered round me sometimes, all scribbling and laughing away while I punched in the front-line information: MR HARRISON HAS GOT GINGER PUBES; MICHELLE COWLEY IS A COW. They're a great crowd at work. Even when I went to the pub, room was always made for me and my crutches. It was like I was sat at the centre of a wonderful dream.

At night, I slept in a velvet pit, all smiles while my leg had a hug in its cast. The clean lines of my crutches really pleased me up against my white wood-chipped walls, really added to my exterior, and, when I was out playing really hard somewhere, I leaned on the snug black leather cushions tucked under my arms like I was leaning into more of me. They proved quite useful as well. Sometimes, after some hard play, I'd be drawn up to Katy and Tracy's flat, especially after a couple of pints, and that's when the combination of heavy plaster, two crutches and two essentially caring nurses paid off. As the flat is five flights up, by the time I'd slogged up there I'd usually be covered, dripping, actually, in sweat, and if Katy and Tracy were in (which they were as I'd see them get home), then, well, they could hardly turn me away on my crutches. I felt really close to Katy especially, like she was my spiritual twin, like we'd got separated at birth, and what I found I wanted, more than anything else, was to lie straight down on that couch again. Like, get in touch with my centre, be intensively cared for once more. One night it was pretty great there because I got to eat pizza with them and watch a video. Tracy even called me a taxi. At the door I told her she has 'great eyes', even though she's got eyes like pins. Birds love a random compliment.

Unfortunately, my hospital appointment to have my plaster taken off threatened to cut off my dream. In the morning Mum kept giving me the white appointment card as I hopped off to work. I was looking forward to having that plaster removed like I'd look forward to having a head amputation. Mum kept going on about it. I missed the first appointment accidentally on purpose, and it got deferred for a week. Then I missed that one as well.

Eventually, Mum calls the doctor round to the house herself. Apart from her being annoyed with me for clumping about on the ceiling, the hospital really want those crutches back and keep phoning up. I tell the doctor I'm prepared to buy them off him myself, like pay, I whisper, cash, but he wasn't having any of that. In fact he went into a bit of a rant about chipping and cutting at the NHS, about bloody users / sponges / leeches / time-wasters, the usual stuff, but, as he was holding this spinning wheel drill thing over my leg at the time, it all got a bit scary. To calm him down I tell him he's got 'healing hands'. Compliments don't really work on blokes. He broke the plaster in front of me, which was annoying as I was actually planning to re-use it again.

The sight of my leg after the plaster came off was horrible, quite a shock. Compared with the other one, it was all withered and scaly. Mum said it reminded her of me next to Helen in the incubator. When I scratched it, my skin flaked off. It was horrible. It was like my black carpet had dandruff. I oiled the leg down and then, brainwave, as it felt quite fragile, I wound bandages around it all the way past my ankle. I even rolled my suit trousers up a bit so it got noticed at work. That was OK for the first couple of days, but then all the little attentions I got from having the plaster on in the first place wore off. At the coffee percolator it was strictly Pour the Coffee and Go. The Marketeers, well, when I approached their circle in the pub, that seat or this seat was always taken, so it got a bit tough going standing up at the bar.

At home, well, to cut a long story short, it was like the long autumn and winter of my discontent. The backdrop really got to me. If it wasn't snowing it was raining kind of thick mud. I had one fluffy-hair day after another. I lay on my bed listening to my jazz CDs, but actually, without the weight of the plaster, I began to feel a bit light-headed, like the notes were like worms in my eardrums, making me feel quite nauseous. Dizzy and annoyed. Jazz is quite a discordant noise. I don't think I really like it that much. My leg throbbed as well. I wrapped the bandages even tighter but it still kind of bleated. At work I got noticed for making a mess and got called to head office twice. Yelled at. That Gary Kiblin kept leaping onto my desk, flapping his black suit jacket over his head like wings, like he was a vulture and I was the dead stinking bit of meat already. At home, I lay on my bed and played my electric guitar or played jazz really loudly just in case Katy and Tracy rang. They didn't. Mum and Dad banged on the ceiling and Dad came in a couple of times and took all my plugs.

I got to go to a couple of parties after that, but I think, around then, I must have caught post-viral/broken-leg syndrome or something. It was quite an effort standing in the hall at parties. For a while I got off on 'Great dress', and, when the bird started thinking perhaps that was too personal a comment, like too close to her precious naked skin, I'd say, 'My girlfriend's got one the exact same.' Or I'd whisper, at super-emergency compliment time, 'It suits you much better.'

I got myself up to Katy and Tracy's flat quite a few more times, against quite a depressing backdrop of slurpy snow. If Tracy, Nurse Ratchet-Features, opened the door though, well, it's like I'd get to see her and the inside of the flat for about one second. That bird could turn sugar sour, whole hay lofts full of apples, cure diabetes. I'd hate to be her patient. She's got fat arms as well. 'Nice jumper,' I said, just as the door slammed.

If Katy answered though, well, she's a bit of a soft touch – especially as I often had a fluffy toy or something, a flower behind my back. She'd jump a bit with surprise. A couple of times I got to sit with her while she made herself ready for work. I'd see her in her nurse's uniform, but actually, I don't know why people go on about them being sexy or something, because actually they're like blue sacks. Katy, if anything, got more businesslike in her uniform. Quite abrupt and bossy. She went on about how hard nursing is, how they need time to unwind, as if I don't. Like my job's easy. I switched off a bit while her mouth worked. Her hair though, above the bland uniform, was really great to look at. Haloed. When I was back in my bed I'd dream I was brushing it, or I was a tiny thing lying in it, like a flea or a kirby grip really gripping in tight.

+

Well, to cut a long story short, it turned out Mum and Dad had been planning to emigrate to Australia for quite some time. They sprang this news on me suddenly. They weren't planning on taking me with them either. Ms God Almighty, Helen, was on the phone braying day and night and vice versa. One day I came home from work and found a red FOR SALE sign in our front garden. A month later a SOLD sign was slapped over that. Suddenly, I'm in a robot clearing hall. Crates were packed. Lists made, ticked and crossed off. Mum and Dad were really humanoid, fully switched on. I was going to be homeless. I had to keep mouthing that to myself to make it true. *My name is Tony Wornel and I am going to be homeless.* Then, it *was* true. I waved my parents off at Heathrow and off they flew, away. I only had a couple of weeks to find somewhere else to live. At work, it was back to my squirrelling days. Tony Wornel punching in his information. I really wanted to get lifted out of myself. Be Tone out partying, having a chat. I tied my support bandages on really tight and let the pavement convey me whither. I was trying to stay really open to the possible.

One night I followed these two birds holding a bottle of wine into a house, and that's how I got the black eye. Unfortunately, that was on a Friday night. By Monday morning it was gone completely so nobody could make a fuss at work, or like get me a card.

It was quiet in the house. Not nice 'n' quiet. More like a water torture noise in a tomb. When I couldn't bear that kind of quiet any·more I pressed the redial button on my fax–phone. Katy and Tracy rarely answered it. Then an answerphone answered, and after the bleep I found myself suspended right above the possible. I heard all this static in my ear. Like the static was *inside* me. Crackling. Like I was listening to an echo of my interior. Quite frightening. Then I realized it was just me breathing.

Each night I'd take a long short cut home from work and sit outside Katy and Tracy's flat re-winding the bandages on my leg. I was hoping Katy and Tracy would see me and come down and help, or, better yet, invite me up to their flat for a chat. Their window looked really steamed-up and cosy, full of warm yellow light. I imagined they were eating pepperoni pizza and walking around in their half slips, smoking French fags, and arguing about whose hotels were on New Bond Street. I was supposed to be out looking for a bedsit.

Then I got this bedsit on Downs Park Road (no view of the downs though) and, without much ado, well, none, I moved in. As I said, my chrome and black leather looks pretty stupid in here. The walls *and* the ceiling have been papered, more like peppered over, with poppy wallpaper. Waking up in the mornings the poppies look like bloody, messy bullet holes.

I've decided to sell all my electric wizardry before some bastard nicks it.

One night I knocked on Katy and Tracy's door after I'd drunk a few too many in the Bar Lorca. I got really depressed in the Bar Lorca. I couldn't work on my conversational gambits as the music was too loud and it was that Latin stuff that worries away at your solar plexus. At the bar it was like I was speaking an underwater language or something and this Irish bird kept laughing at everything I said. And these couples were spinning around making me feel sick. Anyway, I managed to get into Katy and Tracy's flat by crying, and at first I'm really putting it on so I can get to sit on that couch and get looked after, but then I really *am* crying. I peeped through my fingers and explained (lying a bit) I was going to be homeless soon and could I stay on their couch. I saw Katy falter but that bitch Tracy was in there straight away. Quite rude as well, the fat cunt. She practically got me by the collar and threw me out. 'Nice shoes,' I managed, as the door slammed.

Anyway, to cut a long story short, last night I got up there again. I'd already tripped up on the pavement as my support bandage had come undone, so my nose was bleeding. I didn't clear the mess up though, as I thought it might reactivate Katy's slack caring hormones. Tracy was at work. (I'd made sure of that.) I'd bought a new chrome suitcase. I thought, If I could just get my tartan toothbrush in between theirs, I could get my exteriors sorted again. I'm good with exteriors. I should have just stuck with that. And I thought how great it would be living with two birds. Like midnight chats. Like videos and guitar-playing and reading magazine knowledge out loud. I was having those kinds of fantasies when Katy opened the door. Her bottom lip went all quivery when she saw me. Quite emotional. She really did look like an angel. The hall light was shining through her frizzy hair. She looked quite celestial. I stated my case, so to speak. I got my foot through the door, sniffing back a large black blood bubble, when suddenly there's this big bloke standing in front of me. He says, 'I'll handle him, Kate.' I say, 'Whoa, great muscles, do you work o—'

Compliments don't really work on blokes. When I wake up I'm in a hospital ward but I'm feeling no pain. This nurse tells me I'll have to wear this neck brace for about six months. *And* I've busted my femur bone again. Well, I couldn't be happier. I'm really feeling full of the possible. 'Mantula,' I say, reading this nurse-bird's name tag, passing into Unconscious Land. 'Hey, *un*usual name.'

Kissing Time

She said, when she could, 'How long have I got?' The dentist's assistant wheeled away disgusted. The dentist was young. He had alopecia (now that wasn't fair, was it?), head like a kid's fight, the damage combed over, his fingers in latex, the smell of new dollies. A hosepipe, the smell of something a long, long time rotting. She lay back, cried . . . The noise was tremendous: spluttering scraping, needles. Needles of light. The dentist was yelling, 'Quite frankly, young lady, never never never in my life . . .'

The dentist yelled, 'What did I tell you, I told you, use short vibratory movements . . . the surfaces . . . not always possible . . . clean between, up and down, *not* slash . . . *Floss* . . .'

Seven feet of floss across the bathroom floor, in the bin, floss webs. On the sink, teeth paraphernalia: dental gum, interdental gum picks, angled toothbrushes. Anti-plaque gargle gargle gag. Too much, too bloody late. Blood in the toothpaste, rinse, gag, soft gums. Blood on the skin of an apple.

Oh God, her teeth. She was going to lose her teeth.

With a tan they'd flash across four hundred yards. In winter packed and beige—

She smoked, they were purple behind (the dentist said, 'Oh for Christ sakes look! *Look!*'), like curd in Chinese restaurants, and sometimes, like underneath her nails.

The gums were receding, going nowhere fast.

Outside the dentist's the heat was a white glass sheet. Dusty cars blared their horns at traffic jams, fingers drummed roofs. She wanted to run crazy and smash the heat with her hands. She stumbled into a bleached-out park, fell on a bench and fell, instantly, apart. She saw her mother's dentures floating with a fat blue fly. She saw her father smile with his lips held taut, like his plate would spin out and into space. She saw old soft collapsed faces sitting out in deckchairs, their legs far apart. Her father yelled, 'Say *Cheese!*' and photographs reeled away from her: two and a half decades of smiles.

Twenty-five years old: down to bone.

No one would kiss her.

In the park, in the no-breeze, it hit her: no one would kiss her. No one would kiss her. She saw lovers in swimsuits. She saw kissers everywhere, kissing. She saw her face turned up and her lids going down like blinds. The air thickening. She felt emotions load in her chest and launched herself home.

No one would kiss her with false teeth.

Bare chests burned in her road. Diggers dug over yellow pipes and tubes, machines spun. A tiny red radio blared, not tuned in, a crackling disturbance in the air. She stamped up the pavement. She smelt toffee-apple tarmac and tea stewing in a little toothpaste-coloured hut. 'Cheer up my darling,' a big one said. She chose him. She walked up to him, so close his smile slipped. 'Come on then,' she said, 'Come on then. *Kiss.*'

His name was Phil. She could call him Philly. She could call him anything she liked, my doll. She took him from his little hut, down the road to her room. His mates screamed. His mates could not believe his luck.

She was twenty-five, only twenty-five.

She pulled the curtains shut and pulled in for the close-up: he had little black hairs in groups poking out of his nose and four pulled-apart pores. His big rough hands were on her back, stirring it, feeling for a strap. She knew, seconds before his lips clamped hers, his tongue would be a slug and also have the texture of liver. Four out of five were like that: meat in their mouths.

But he was – gentle, his bottom lip soft and feeling like a bruise.

She lay in bed counting up all the men she'd kissed.

When it was dawn and grey stripes had come through the blinds and the house martins were at it and the car alarms were going off and Phil was still, heavily, asleep, she counted up all the boys, including kiss chase.

She saw two, then one . . . an identical twin called Antony. She'd identify him by the birthmark on his knee in the shape of England and his bright yellow cable-knit cardi. He was blond and brown and ran away from her. She had longer legs.

She ran to get him ready or not. He was never ever ready. He hid. He was a giant canary in a tree. She shook him down, pursued without mercy. 'KISS ME NOW!' she'd yell across the playground. She saw the sweet white spit on his lip, the tremble in it, the way his skin was polished. And he cried straight afterwards, fists balled in his eyes.

Jase. He beat up on anything small, insects, smaller boys. He had no mercy. He was thin and hard and fast like a grey-hound (he probably died in a motorcycle crash, or a fire in a disco, something. young). He smoked No. 6 in the palm of his hand, scrunched his face round it. He grabbed her on a school trip, in the Ghost Train. By mistake, he stuck the tip of his tongue up her nose. She had to guide it into her mouth with her finger. They both looked at each other. Eight eyes. A skeleton, luminous monsters, creaked out. Ancient mechanics cackled. Then, he took his tongue away. And never spoke to her or went near her again.

Phil rolled over with a snort, pinning her right leg down. His hand kneaded the spare on her thigh. His mouth was slack, open, wet. She leant up on one elbow for an in-depth look. Not fair, still had all his gums, not fair, big square, deeply rooted teeth, four metal fillings.

She fell back on the pillows, floated off. Boys and men jogged past her eyes, mouths smudged like charcoal.

Duncan, French-kissed like a lizard and McDermod who sucked on her neck till it hurt, who gave her a necklace of bites she wore under shiny polo neck jumpers. Her friends said, 'Been babysitting have we?' And Ian 'monster' Sky whose nice eyes and nice lips lay on a carpet of spots, but who wiggled when he walked, snake hips, who had 'pull'. They'd snog at the top of her road, she'd run home straight after, show him the soles of her shoes, and gargle and scrub her face with medicated soap as though the pustules had split and were taking over her face like something crazy from Space.

Spud. Serious and quiet, a medical student, he liked his white coat, wore it on dates, pretended he'd forgotten he was wearing it. His fountain pens pressed on her breasts. He treated her mouth like a cleaned-out wound, lips working out the neatest cross-stitch.

Bill. A wide mouth, teeth like a set from a dolphin. Smoked, his tongue like an emery board under water, the gaps in his teeth sedimented and sour, he could do it for hours. The stubble on his face made her chin red so her dad turned away from her and all her friends knew 'what you've been doing'.

Jimmy. No lips, the nipper, fastidious. He wouldn't put his tongue in her. She didn't want his tongue in her. He nipped and bit. He didn't like a mess, he didn't like anything wet. He did as much as he had to and no more.

Dick. Like his name. The grabber. He'd lunge for her neck, fistful of hair and tear her to him. Pulled her into his mouth, all of her, ankles and feet disappearing.

Harry. Urgent in the nose, he'd make snorting noises, he went straight down her throat, dirty and fast.

John. Spend hours on the approach, first one eye, then the

other eye, then cross-eyed, the space he'd eat between their mouths, make it like a long neck-nuzzling horse.

And, alone at a party, seriously drunk, her hair and body damp with dancing, she wiggled around a strobe-lit room. Turning a corner someone with no name pulled her up against a wall, roughly and dryly moved all over her face. She felt a beard, wiry. It was all – rude. Left her without breath, spun on the wall.

It wasn't a long list really, mostly boys. No one would kiss her with false teeth, no one.

She stood in Philly's vest, it smelt of concrete dust, dried yellow-onion sweat, brushing at her teeth. Outside, she heard the diggers vibrating the road. Vibrations tingled under her toes. The mirror was old and tinted and flattered the mesh of her hair and her distant face. The toothpaste gave her a foaming smile. She looked rosy, young. She was too young . . . could not happen to her. Her eyes swam. She tasted blood down her throat. Phil pinched her, said, 'Well girly, got to hit the road,' grinned, his reflection big and brown and black, his body hair a scrawl of acrylic, his body stuffed too full with blood, like the colour stuffed in a horse. You wouldn't think he could kiss. You wouldn't think that at all.

She kissed him. She wouldn't let him go. She followed him down the hall. He said, 'Hey, let go . . .'

She was only twenty-five.

She hadn't kissed properly yet. He said 'Oy, *get* . . .'

She followed him down the road to work.

Shop Talk

She was pulling out Hoover coils. 'Well, he just goes into a moody so I think . . .'

'I'm not joking, his eyes bored into me like that snake in *The Jungle Book.*'

In the back of the shop the click of the kettle, coffee clouds, the gold crusts of microwaved croissants. Quarter of an hour before the soundtrack reeled on. Sal drew on a wide purple mouth.

'What did you do last night, Sal?'

'TV. Dinner. Bed.' Fight.

+

Loll's armchair. Her couch.

In the bathroom her toiletries on two packed shelves, some of them gluey and furred with dust. Some of them laced together with cobweb. He saw a spider strung between a Vosene bottle and an exfoliating skin cream, short, iron trapezing legs. His toothbrush and electric shaver. His toothbrush and electric shaver took up four square centimetres. 'Four square centimetres.'

'If you're measuring I'd make that two,' she leered.

He laughed. But thought: You bitch. And took that thought to work.

+

And crushed it with a spanner, under a Nissan's dark low troubled sky. Twisted it round a nut. 'And suddenly, she's wearing *panda* slippers.' He rolled out on his back, looked up through the sheen of navy-blue covered yard, at Steve in his goggles, flame-throwing wrecks. The silhouettes of his springy mustard-cress hair. 'What ja think, Steve?'

Steve said, 'Chuck her.'

+

'That really suits you.' Sal ran the back of a hand down the rack of Ghost, Nicole Farhi, French Connection, Sturgeon, the corral of alarm-rich black leather shirts. All day she galloped round in faux fur boots, tilting like a pretty seahorse, whacked by texture, colour, sounds. By four o'clock, shaking with caffeine, they all went really, really mad to Gypsy Kings, running in and out of the changing rooms, plaiting their hands in front of their faces like four Björks. She loved working here. Dressing up as a different woman every day.

She wrote lyrics on the back of paper bags. She sounded so great in her pink soapy bath. Hair piled up like a sparkly cone of vanilla ice cream.

+

'I've always loved, don't know why,' Steve said, holding up a flaking orange socket spanner, 'short, you know, fat girls.'

+

'Mmm,' said the customer, wriggling down a pink sausage skin, 'do you think it makes my bum look too wide?'

Yes, Sal thought. 'No. It *really* suits you . . . That'll be four hundred and seventy-five pounds.'

'That'll be a month's mortgage and a trip to Safeway's.'

'Bye now, don't forget your receipt.'

She had to swallow hard sometimes. Tongue dry. Like she was going to cry. She wrote on a gold-sprayed paper bag: 'Surrounded by plenty baby, baby, tears in my throat, la la la.'

'He came in, right, said he'd like to try it on as he happened to be *exactly* the same size as his wife. Looked straight at me. I looked *straight* back.'

'What you doing tonight, Sal?'

'Dinner. Video. Pub.' Fight.

She saw Loll on his armchair, scowling.

+

Steve said, 'Wear two condoms from now on. Once it gets domestic . . .'

Domestic. It rang in his head.

'Once she, she washed my overalls, right. Couldn't *stand*

71

that. Like she'd efffing wiped me out . . .' Years of wiping oil and brown grease on his thighs so they caked, each day like slipping pale fuzzy legs through a map of himself. Saw his overalls sloshing up against the glass bright blue. 'I don't effing *believe it*.'

'I couldn't get this *particular* stain out, Loll,' she'd said, pointing out one left. From a Laguna he'd skinned down in January '92.

He'd had to sit back on the couch like he'd been whacked.

He'd go home and clear her the hell out. Her three wardrobes and ten shelves. His one chrome bar. Her . . .

+

'. . . Love me baby, aha aha, as I am . . .'

'Tofu? It's like thigh fat that tofu stuff, innit. Like eating someone else's cellulite.'

+

He fiddled in the innards of a crushed silver Golf GTI, eyes half shuttered like a vet's, moving his oiled and corded forearm round like he was easing a calf out: slipping it through two wet clenched cow walls. He blinked through the subterranean gloom, through the scorched plastic double take of his goggles, saw, with a grin, Steve skim the stained ocean floor. 'Yo. *Yo!*' In the gates, in a pale lozenge of yellow sunshine, two chubby schoolgirls clicked past. Steve cooing lewd, 'Babies. Yo there, baby dolls.'

Loll grinning, shaking his head like a suede dog.

+

'I'm not joking, I read about it in a book. It's a test. You throw them . . .' she whispered, '*your knickers*, like pasta, up against the wall.' She rang up the till, threw in a bag a parachute of silk. 'If they stick, you fancy him. If they don't, well; you're just drunk.'

A mauve Donna Karan sheath dress sheathed in plastic near the till. £595. She touched it all day, reverently slipped her hand in for its cool inside, the frisson it gave her silk palm, sending her reeling out with the lunch list from throbbing Seal into the blowy silent-by-comparison high street. Feeling a kind of pleasant anguish as though someone were about to lift up her hair, shiver-kiss her neck. The chill of the fruit counter in M&S, holding four tuna fish with mayo on brown; apricots, a lemon fruit spritzer they'd drink in champagne glasses for lunch.

+

A hush round it. Spotlit in the centre of the yard. Seagull doors. Glassed-in lights. Walnut panelling. Expensive perforated tack. He slid inside the lilac upholstery, breathed in Turtle Wax, the intimate scent of new car: one expensive – from the stub in the ashtray – briefly smoked cigar. He pulled on the wristy gears. Grunt from the engine. Brand new and the fucker wouldn't start. Palmed his groin down hard. Pushed in an ancient CD. Madness. 'One Step Beyond'.

Pushed his head through the sun roof mouthing, 'ONE STEP BEYOND.' Had a dance about before lunch, stamping boots through petrol-coloured puddles. Felt joy briefly kick in. And kick out. Slumped over his pineapple juice in the pub.

'Eat up,' Steve said, eating, mash on his tongue.

'Can't. Full up.'

+

'They videoed the birth.'

'No!'

'Yes! Video *nasty*! When she tore you could hear it on the Sony. Like, have you ever ripped rotten sheets really quickly?'

+

'*Fuck!*' A piss-spurt from an oil tank blacked his eye. Laughing. Their laughter ran up like rodents and bellowed off the tiles. Listening, head back, to the last echo notes, he heard Sal squeech away in the bath. And felt for her a little, leaky, belly-ache of warmth.

+

'Should babies wear make-up?'

'No, if they're ugly. No. Like – *that one last week, urgh!*'

They stood in the corner, gagging, panting after a Gypsy Kings workout. She looked at them, at their white leather sheaths, brightly coloured hair. She must look just like them.

74

Shop girls. Mutant fruits. A quick feeling of revolt. A revolting feeling.

'Fruit sisters, yeah, we are fruit . . .'

End of day. Setting the alarm. Keying in her birth date and half of Loll's. Something de-tagged, rolled up tight beneath her arm.

+

Day over. Locking the garage door with Steve, a quick game of noughts and crosses in the dotty grime between thick, blackly oiled crossbars. He won. Walking, loosened, home.

'Nice day, Sal?'

She was cutting up a pineapple on the crowded kitchen table, her back to him, shaped like an egg-timer in a new mauve dress. 'Yeah, not bad. Yours?'

He quickly assessed. 'Yeah, 'bout 'same. Hey, Sally girl.' She turned round. 'You're looking . . . er, well, good.' He grinned. 'Why don't you, um . . . get over here?'

Old Times

They didn't write each other letters, or phone much. If you're solid for life you don't have to do much. And they were blood brothers. They had thumb scars, white, raised, four-year-old little bleeders, screaming down the garden path. Their mums had gone, 'Oh Christ!' Thirty-five years ago. They didn't have to write or ring, but once a year they had a right weekend of it, down Rick's place, down the smoke. Len got on the train, swung past Rugby and Nuneaton with his Tennent's Extra and his instant mates in the mini-bottle beverage bar. In his flat, Rick straightened his cushion and his tie, all ready, set.

All the years before they drowned The Big Weekend in a sea of beer and wine, and beached, fish-eyed on the Monday, Rick teaching a riotous assembly God knows what, Len touting his cassette round the Go Away Clubs. They always had a great time. Gra-*ate!* Even though they could hardly remember it.

Thirty-nine. Nearly forty year old.

Friday night, they kept it local. And did their double act

'eh upping' and 'thou lassing', and shot games of pool in the pub. And woke up with the living room thick with sock. 'Don't you *ever* wash . . .' Rick said, holding his nose, flapping. 'Don't start,' Len yelled, a wrinkled mole in the couch, 'starting.'

They looked at each other drop-jawed. They'd never got off on the wrong note before.

Six forty-five a.m. Saturday morning. Dehydrated. Might as well stay up, get an early start. Outside, dirty sparrows peeped on the glass. Outside, solid silver banks of cloud scrolled past. Outside a mad man screamed KILL ME KILL KILL KILL . . . Inside, Len said, 'How you can fuking live here, fuk.' Rick said, 'Jobs.' Then he said, 'I meant nothing . . .' He said, 'Lenny? Fuk sake's . . .' He put Elvis on, toast on, the kettle on and soon (after a smoke), the humpy bump was smoothed. Soon, they were well ripped, heeheeing side by side, being little with the bleedy knife. 'Oh, Mammy,' they said together, 'we're blee-dy!' They said together, 'Oh Chroist!'

In the hall, biting gum, they squared up at the mirror. And froze over gap-toothed combs. The mirror squared back. Both had long lost their looks. Both were losing their hair. Both had pink skin-skids on top. The skids had got loads wider since last year's. Both thought, Gord, he looks rough. 'Why-we're-looking-gra-ate!' Len lied, like a (third-division) football manager. They paused. The pause went, they raised thumbs, hee-heed, and went out.

It was lovely and sunny outside, bright blue and breezy.

Bright blue blasts of air. They raced down the high street like centre forwards, did headers into shops, tapped nifty finger work on their cashpoint cards: four saved-for hundred pounds for one major big bang bash. 'Show this country boy a good time,' Len yelled. He threw himself on the windows of cake shops like Spider-Man and puffed out clouds. In there were, ah, jail bait. In there were hard-faced girls one-gloved like gynos. In there were girls who still blew up their bubblegum. In there . . . 'Nay lad,' said Rick, he dragged Len's collar, 'Nay. Away. Let's not peak too soon.'

They raced to the bus stop. The bus stop swayed away in The Waste. Here, it was sad, bad, mad. Here, the stalls were chocker with dead men's cordless dressing gowns. Miscellaneous bankrupt stock walled the street. Knackered black girls and knackered white girls clip-clopped home from clubs. Len sucked the smoke out of a fag in one drag, his eyes glittered like maniacs'. 'Fuking cor,' he said, 'fuking cor-ish.' 'Do you think this is me?' Rick said, holding up a shirt, swirly, not his normal brown. 'No,' said Len. 'Oh,' said Rick. 'Ooh,' said Len, 'Ooh ooh I feel like, I feel . . .' He was straining like a baby shits. Rick knew that look. 'Oh Christ,' he said to Christ, 'not—' But it was far too late. 'SINGING,' sang Len. With a flash he had a finger in his ear and was warbling, with confidence, through 'Candle in the Wind'. Two of Rick's pupils sniggered past. A crowd coagulated: a yellow-eyed frothy-mouthed hound and a bag lady with black teeth. Rick thought, Oh dear, what shall I do? He gummed support, hummed, and tried to vault a passing astral plane. The bag lady unravelled rags to her own larly-la rave-on, while a nasty thought raved in Rick's ear, and pulled him right back down: Len really thinks he'll get discovered, it's dead embarrassing. A drink-blurred memory stirred: Mind, it was right embarrassing last year when . . . '*Don't* take that off, lady, fuk's sake,' Len yelled and he grabbed Rick's head and banged a tunnel with it through the crowd.

At 10 a.m. they were losing at the dogs. As the hare slid round, Rick said, 'Lenny, the yelling's new. What's with the yelling? *Eh, Lenny . . . ?*' At 11 a.m., three hundred quid short, they double-decked it to town and did the galleries. At 11.30 a.m. they shared a loaded pipe in Green Park and a six-pack of really strong lager each. At 11.45 a.m. Rick said, 'Lenny, do you ever feel . . .' He went on at length . . . 'cut out, bored, do you ever feel that this is *all* there is?' He was looking up through the rusting lace of a tree. Disabled pigeons dangled long white strings of shit. The sky had gone blueless. 'Nay lad,' said Len. He cracked a can, 'London's done yer, there's loads. There's er, songs, doggies, footy, curry yeah and – birds.'

High noon: they were rowing on the Serpentine. The water was a thick grey carpet with ruffled-up underlay. 'I don't know,' said Rick, gasping, 'me spark's gone. Sometimes I feel just like a song . . . No, I mean . . .' But, too late, Len was cued on. Soon, splashes. Soon ten old, hardy, sparsely covered heads bobbed alongside the boat. Ten heads hummed on Len's voice. Swans and geese rose up in protest. Rick winced the boat round. Twice he begged, 'Please

Lenny oh please stop . . .' but Lenny cracked on: Paul Simon. And Garfunkel, Barry Manilow, Elton John. He started in on Sinatra, stood up to wheel about with the mike. He rocked the boat. He rocked it again. Slimy water sloshed in. Then tipped Rick and Len in. Right in. Everything went frozen and thick and quiet and deep and a deathlike grey.

At – whatever time it was, they'd lost track, they sat in shock, in the dank boat house, peeled and steaming over a tiny candle flame. Their damp green blubber loomed up at each other . . . a distant memory: Trafalgar Square, fountain, same thing, tipped in, soaked, last year. Rick said, 'I remember why you . . . you . . . fuk fuk fuk . . .' He remembered more from years before. He wanted to say a whole lot more. His jaw cha-cha-cha-chattered but nothing else came out. 'Drink,' Len managed, his lips belched up . . . three, tiny black-gold fish.

Blinkless, they sat, crammed in a Soho pub, in matching electric blue shell suits (bought, from the bold-faced boatman, for the fat, wet, almost-end of their cash). Their bits of hair scribbled on their scalps, their toes squelched in nylon socks, in green plastic flip-flops. Whiskies and gingers funnelled through their chests. 'My life,' Rick said, 'well, our lives actually, flashed in front of me like – that,' he snapped his shrivelled pads, 'and it weren't nothing much . . . then all I saw were wiggly old legs.' He went on, 'We're nearly forty year old . . .' 'Burger,' Len said, 'get me . . . suet pudding, curry. Chips. Fat yellow . . .'

They tumbled out under a low old-bruise-coloured sky:

ravenous, wrecked, they tumbled over stubble grass. Sinking, they ate in shadows, in Soho Square. The smell of hot vinegar soon drew crowds. Bony girls circled them, begging. People who fell over a lot held out scabby hands. 'This is fuking horrible,' Len said, hugging his chips, 'don't remember this from last year.' 'Me neither and I live here but hey, maybe *we died*,' Rick said, he looked dead cheered up, 'maybe we're in Limboland, maybe . . .' 'Maybe you got a crack on the fuking head,' Len yelled, '*de*-pressing git.'

And soon it was black. Winter black and neon and car lamps and shop fronts cubed the streets: pink, yellow, blue, pink and yellow, black. Leather leaves and shiny rags from porn mags stuck on their shell suit legs. They rustled down a sex street in the aftermath of a row – their first since last year's big bang bash or was it . . . the big bang bash before that? Lightning grievances flashed. Loaded four eyes aimed, triggered, backfired. Both thought: this is well not fun, exactly like last year . . . or, well, was it the year before that? Rick looked at his flapping flip-flopped feet. Len couldn't help it, he just looked. His neck was a pivot turning his head into bed shows. From doorways leopard-skinned girls crooked their figures and their smiles. Len drooled, made like – Rick pulled on his collar. 'We don't want to peak too . . .' 'I do,' snapped Len. 'Fuk off.' And he raced down to play down-down with the leopards.

'And um, don't come back,' Rick said, all alone on the yellow, grey, blackening street.

Hours of packed sleaze-horror slewed by.

Rick dropped his jaw as instant mates beat him up. In an alley, Rick was held, sweating, screaming, upside down, the electric blue arms of his shell suit were ripped off, his soft parts squeezed, change gushed like a simultaneous win on two fruit machines from his deeply pocketed legs. (But, no flies on him, none: a damp tenner lay curled like an embryo, inside a sock.) Released, Rick waited, bleeding at bus stops, but no buses would stop. Coagulating, he limped along bus routes, his old, homey, thumb scar bleat bleat bleating distress.

By – and it was only 7.30 p.m. Knackered. And, it was Cahrist, fuking Saturday night! Rick was turning the handle to his flat. His hands and his bones were so heavy. His body ached. Tears shone on his face like two twists of cellophane. Ah, the couch to stay on, age on, collapse. He went for it but the hallway caught him short; assailed his nose with Radox and old, warm, over-painted radiators, a familiar Bisto curl of sock. 'Len?' Len came out of the bathroom, his face cut up and bloodied up. 'Snap,' he said. They both said, flat, 'We're bleedy, oh Chroist.' After a wobble, Len said, 'Er, what d'ya think my son . . . we get a curry . . . we stay in? Er, early night? Vid . . . ?

'Er, Rick?'

'Nay,' said Rick, 'Nay. *Away.*' They rushed out.

Gabriel Ascending

When I used to drink I'd fall over like a baby. Lovely. Never feel a thing. This fellow – Dave? Mark? Den? – he'd get me here. I'd always wake up here.

This fellow at the AA. This fellow . . . He looked like a priest – wore an ankle-length black coat, face above it, clear blue skin, popped blue eyes, like he'd never had a drink in his life. Or been out in a bit of weather. This fellow who *was* the AA. Your original, radiant, Born Again. His real name? We called him Gabriel, Gabby, Gabs. For? Descending on drinkers and giving out gyp. Each meeting he'd drag along a new one and while outside in the main hall the ping-pong balls were pinging back and forth and these matrons were giving the floorboards a bit of 'ooh' and bounce, he'd be inside, whispering and urging, using their rhythm, trying to get the poor shaking fool to say it, what he or she is: a wretch. I've said it myself. He's how I came here myself.

His method? Simple. He'd spy you quietly sipping or in the act of falling over or catching a kip, sunbathing in the

85

rain, in the park, and then, he would not let you go. You'd look up and there he is and you'd look up and there he is and the next thing you're here, propped up, bleating on this chair.

But not—It did not work on Gina. This woman he brought along, Gina. This woman, his live-in love. You could tell they were—And you could tell he'd been working on her and his angel act was just about doing her in. He dragged her here just once and she was just one *rude* . . . We all perked up. Leopard-skin coat, a sight of some kind of furry black sheath underneath; tripping towards our little crew on these high red shoes. She wore her drink vapours like a heady perfume. No ruination evident. A dish and a bit. A miserable dish and a bit. While he was urging she was biting her bottom lip till I wanted to beg her don't you hurt it and she was scraping the paint off a nail and one hand was up her smoky locks and the other tugged an earring, and all the time he was right behind her squeezing his wings. But, he couldn't squeeze one bleat out of her. Lovely. Lovely to see. At the tea urn, during the break, a couple of us were grinning and the atmosphere was all genial and light.

At the next two meetings though, he's not there. And at the next two meetings, he's not there and it's not the same without him. It's kind of chatty, but it's not the same. He was holier-than, but it kind of worked.

Just not on Gina. (I still dream about Gina.) I saw her one streaming black night, stumbling, screaming out of a pub, hands on hips, abuse-abuse, then clicking down the street in her high red shoes. And there was Gabriel descending, whispering and urging, being everywhere where she looked up. She looked up, 'Davey,' (or Mark, Den), 'ah, please, pa-leeze have a drink.' I thought: Oh dear me no, Gina, he'll get you. Oh yes he will.

Oh no he won't.

He fell. But, he did not fall like me.

My fall? Simple. I miss one meet then something happens and there I am one day with a glass and the next day, magic, it's a drink. Time goes fast – it's a wind machine tossing off a calendar. I don't give giving up, Gabriel, one more thought till I'm fairly rough, one of them shall-I-rain? monochrome days, and I'm in the park sipping, sunbathing, though it's cold and the sky's a rattling metal sheet and the willow trees have blown up skirts and the ducks are getting blasted about on the pond and the swans have got a centre parting up their white backsides. I'm thinking that that is a very funny sight indeed, I'm counting up my blessings (could have been born a duck), when who do I see? Gabs. My first thought? Oh Lord no. My second? He looks rough. Exclamation marks all over that thought: Gabriel *looks rough!!*

And the surge that went through me then was not Christian.

He was kipping on a bench, his fingers in a moist blue plait on that lengthy black lap. He'd been there a while – the way the tree debris had settled and the sparrow bopping on his boot. He looked – rough. I was thinking: now, with the addition of ivy he could be one of those green-tinged knocked-down blocks of statues in the cemetery, with a wing missing, half a face. My smile became a sigh. Why? Because the mighty had fallen. Yes, I was feeling a little let down. A little bit sad.

So I let myself sadly and slowly down on the bench arm, got my bottle out and let the wine take different routes down my chin. And soon I was feeling, well, kind of companionable, all the cheery chats we could have now he couldn't flap his wings. I'd leave him a good purple inch. I'd give him a smoke. I'd be good to him and, important, *I would not gloat*. And just like that, as I glugged, I heard my own mother calling and a wee tale she used to tell above my cradle, head sideways on her hand: something about an angel and a mouse. Enough. Just enough for my two tears to let go as the bottle dribbled out. I like a cry. I was just revving up to me bawl when I heard a voice crack, 'Andy, stop that!' and I thought, Ah, ya bastard Gabs, a trap.

No, it wasn't.

The moment I turned my head I could see he had not fallen. He had not fallen down drunk. He was sick. Very. Sweating like he'd been squeezed. His pop eyes had sunk and they'd lost their bright blue blaze, and he'd lost so much weight he was almost one-dimensional. If he stood up he'd be a shadow. He stood up and was. It was like I was walking along talking to myself. What'd he done? She'd gone, 'Gina . . . tiger . . . no, don't go . . .' He'd gone out hunting for her. He slumped along my arm. The one coherent thing he said was could I get him home. He waved a keyring at me – a purple and green globe. I thought, Ah, yes, I remember the world.

Well, I got him home by bus. It was kind of a good idea at the time. I was pissed. There it was wide and red and friendly. He groaned as it jolted over the ruts and ditches in the road and hummed for twenty years in the traffic. And the branches scraping along the juddering sides seemed to scrape inside his soul. No joke. Oh he was groaning and making funny sounds and his neck muscles had turned to mush. I soon explained that. I got my hand inside his pocket (for the bus fares), and pulled out a triple pack of pills. A disease, in Latin, about sixteen names, swam at me, lay gasping on my tongue for a mo, then splashed, tail-end, away. Poor Gabby, oh my poor Gabs. I got my arm around him, gave him a manly squeeze. He groaned. Still, we might have been OK, we might have made it neat and nice, but in the next seat up an ancient fellow (there's always one fellow), puffed on a bugle-sized cigar – kind of defiant. I showed him the size of my fist, but he was one of those World War Oners long past terror. He puffed. The green smoke was a poison whorl. It whirled towards us. I felt Gabby's symptoms for him: the dry heave, the cold sweat, the top of the head wrung out, that runny feeling in the jowls. If you swallow it's – technicolour yawn. Projectiles . . . oh God, it was peas . . . How can a slice of shadow make such a mess?

The bus conductress thumped down through the steamy stench, unbelieving. Gasping, 'Bastards . . . my *bus!*'

I couldn't apologize enough. I couldn't. We were out.

The pavements were made of a bouncing material. It kept giving under my boots and Gabs was half-strung round my neck like a black overcoat on a suddenly hot day. He was babbling, then shouting. I lurched us from lamppost to lamp-post. Fellow pedestrians passed on a firmer path (they must have had a map), swung their heads round on rubber necks and flung us looks registering through disgust. But I couldn't register looks. I couldn't hold on to them.

When I used to drink I'd go with the bounce and a wave of euphoria would whoosh! and the pavement would rush up to greet me in a splendid red kiss. Lovely, like a baby. When you fall you don't . . . You don't feel a thing.

Every time we fell over, I never felt a thing. Gabby though, he felt everything.

His flat. Twenty – somehow, don't ask me – stony flights up. Not how I'd imagined it. Not exactly angelic. I'd thought it would be all bare inside, pin-lighted, aesthetic, black chrome. But no. It was like a junkshop with the lights out: musky chaos, shadows, a wall of lakes, hundreds of dark gold mirrors, some of them cracked. Old food stuck to one of them, a bit of plate. Plus women's clothes, sagging lines of laundry strung across the room. Was it possible – just the one line reflected? Probably. Soap powder, face powder, a mouse-coloured dust billowed over my boots. I stumbled over half-packed suitcases. Ghostly stocking legs kicked me in the face. Somewhere, fountains of books fell down. Gabriel was mumbling over my arm, 'Gina no no no . . . don't go.' I said, 'Shut up.'

Well, I was sick of him. I found the bedroom in a cave and flung him down onto a heap of bed and clothes. I was thinking, wiping off my sweat, Now that is a job really well done. What do I deserve? Gabs was well OK: grunting in the gloom, making kind of pleasant noises, burrowing down deeper like a mole on its back till only the sole of one shoe showed and a socked foot with an immense yellow tower of toe.

I'd never been in such a sexy-messy place. I meant to take his change and leave but my reflections distracted me. Seeing what I looked like from behind, from side to side, distracted me. What would I look like without a beard? I was trying to remember if I had a chin. I went over to the stocking legs and made them kick me again in the face. Lovely. A shelf of pill bottles! I read his name, it was Dave or Mark or Len, one of them. Their primary colours and plastic gleam enticed and, looking for something to wash them down, I opened a cupboard: ten green bottles, almost-empties, sticky lipstick smears. Oh, the flat was a neat division: his crucial medicine; hers. And in my pocket I still had my what-if-it-rains goldy stash. Lovely. From the bedroom I heard Gabby babble on – the beautiful green fields, the gorgeous weather he was having and the marvellous view. Me too, I said and I floated up through the ceiling to heaven.

Oh, I don't know how long. But it was the best time I've had in my life. I came back. A bright spear detached itself from the curtains, hovered for a mo, then bored straight for my head. My hands (when I could look) vibrated at me, green. I was up again, on pulley strings, then down. The first thing I heard was my mother's voice: 'Mmm, cup of tea would be nice,' and instantly, in front of me, a cup of tea formed and sat steaming on its halo. I've never wanted something so much in my life! (That is almost true.) So I watched it, wanting it, for who knows. Then, after the whirligigs, I felt all tingly, happy, off to the kitchen with something to make.

I was halfway to where a kitchen might be, when I remembered, slapped my face (*ouch!*): Gabriel. Gabby, Gabs. Oh no. And not a sound but, outside, a beep, a hoot; a far down traffic jam.

The air in his bedroom smelt brown, bad, tomb bad. In the gloom I saw his shoe, the long yellow toe, but I couldn't hear breathing. I thought, Oh Lordy no. Then, his voice: the faintest rasp through the clothes: 'wonder parks . . . gardens, wonder. Wonder . . . ful flowers . . .' I pulled off some of the clothes and found his face. It was phosphorescent, slightly muzzy, as though he lay underwater, face-up in a pond. A dark growth, a kind of lichen, had sprung up all over his chin. At first I couldn't see how this was possible but he was even thinner than before. Bruises like bruises on old pear skin. I was thinking, now could it be three days? Could I have been . . . no. Was I up there for four? His eyes rolled back and stared up at the new light view. His lips were cracked, dry, but smiling. I heard him whisper, 'fountains . . . water . . .' I heard him definitely croak 'drink'.

I was pouring whiskey down his throat when Gina burst in. She brought in white daylight, a square shaft of light that ran into the bedroom. She stumbled after it, crawling over the suitcases, calling, 'I'm leaving,' and, in a higher, mincey voice, *'and yes I've been drinking.'* She was in that leopard-skin and on the back end of a bender, her black eyes smeared, an old argument boiled away on her mouth. In the white light her skin was lined writing paper, the cheapest. Ruination, alas, was evident. No, I don't think she ever saw me. I think she thought I was a side of furniture, a bit of laundry sagging off a line. She heard. She heard the bottle swill, her lines cleared, she laughed, 'Why, Dave,' (. . . et cetera), 'you're *drinking*!' and then, 'You're *back*!' over and over like he was the one who'd been away. They see-sawed: she hoisted herself up by his shoe; his sole sunk in the stuff of her belly. His sweaty head levered up, down, up. Oh, she was a purring leopard. 'You're *back*!' She sank. Delicious move; her big mouth sank around that yellow toe and – sucked. I thought it was just Gabriel, but it must have been me too: we went, 'Ah, aahhh!' She got to his face. When she got to his face her tongue shot out like a straw for the whiskey splash on his chin. I heard a rattle then, like rattling crockery. In that second he ascended, or the second before. I saw him get up and go up in a white, ankle-length dazzle of coat. And I felt? No, I never felt a thing. I never feel a thing. I was still busy thinking: Mmm, where is it, where's it gone, where's that lovely cup of tea?

Here Comes John

I remember my first one. Nineteen sixty-nine. He was called John. A fine body of a man with his Go on, punch me *right there*, the reddish ripple of muscle, that covering hair. It was all over his stomach and all over his back. It used to crawl over his collar and out of his cuffs. The man was a mat, but I suppose some women must like it. *I* must have liked it. Before my brain grew. And isn't it the way with them, the ones that slap at first, then punch, then give you a right good kicking (keep you straight), it's all mouth. Took him two seconds with drink in him, three without. If I timed it right I could set my tea down steaming and after, after I'd cleared up the mess a bit, it would be just right. Very nice with a fag. And of course he'd be exhausted, fairly whacked, bushed. And it would be, Can't you give me a moment love? (oh, I thought that was one) or Jeezus! You a nymphomaniac or what?

And if you don't learn nothing from that you don't learn nothing.

Cos nothing changes that much does it? The Seventies,

the Eighties, the Nineties. It all boils down to tit men (look at the conkers on that) or cunt men, or leg men. They still like to divide you up. And it don't make no difference if it's squash now stead of rugger, Bacardi not lager, they've all got mental hair on their shoulders, red in the middle, wee white legs. They're still all John. Old John and New John. And even in the Nineties, where it's all talk dirty, they still can't manage it, beckoning you over in a pub with their pinkie and off you trot, ever hopeful, and it's, If I could make you come with my finger think what I could do with my *whole* body. Or they'd spend all evening, and a couple of quid, breathing in your ear even though your hearing's perfect cos they've read some comic says you can do this and it's like foreplay and we won't expect nothing much later. Which brings me nicely round to John.

John was a fine body of a man, all dressed up. My ear would be that wet sitting next to him I'd have to keep swapping places for fear I'd get water on the brain. Now you're probably thinking I'm talking about some motor mechanic or builder as they're usually the ones with the tartan middles and luminous legs, 'cept you'd be wrong. I'm talking about The Johns. The millions of them. They're all stockbrokers, they're all Tories, they're all married (you put a scratch on me I'll lay you out) they're all BORING and so you're probably thinking, so why do you bother and my answer to that is, well, why do you think? Listen. This is how I met John.

Nineteen ninety-three. I was sitting in Rumours under a palm tree nursing a gin and thinking I could jack it all in soon and feeling this cold sore bubbling up on my lower lip, sort of humming, 'Wish I was pretty, Wish I was rich,' when in walks this bloke. Oh-oh, I thought, Here comes John. Oh-oh, I thought, a bit later, fourth gin (not), John reads the *Independent*. Cos it's not all what's a gorgeous bird/chick/bit/ bint doing in an et cetera. It's all uni-this and multilateral-that and IMF and ERM and ECU so you've got to read up a bit for these yuppy Johns and you've got to know your way round shares and things cos they might be tit, cunt and leg men but now they want *brain*. And brain, girls, is what I've got. See this necklace? John got me that. These earrings? John got me that. These shares in British Telecom, British Gas, British Steel, British Airways, British fucking everything, you name it, they sell it, I've got it, cos I bloody well earn it.

So anyways, to cut the eye contact and the, If I could make you come with my et cetera, there's John, finally sitting next to me, soaking my lughole, boring me to sweet Jesus, and I'm doing my Wiggle On The Seat bit (they like you to wiggle, it reminds them of studs and fillies) and to look at me you wouldn't think my brain had just atrophied cos I'm well into automatic and I look interesting. You've got to look interesting! It's all Nineties clean, it's Anneka Rice. So what you need girls is glasses to take off and on, a lot of hair half pinned up and something collarless and well cut and that's me down to a t – with a gin in it. And don't get drunk. Know your limit. He can get legless but you've got to hold your own cos You Need Your Wits About You.

Listen. Here we go.

This is what Johns do. They come straight out with it two seconds before last orders, giving it the old Nigel Havers eyebrow and it's, I feel this strong attraction to you . . . and I think you're an interesting woman but I . . . I better tell you I *am* married. Pause. And then it's the old spaniel 'isn't life cruel' eye dodge and the quicky glance at you cos here's where everything hangs in the balance. This is *the* crucial moment, so watch out girls, watch me girls and *learn* – get it off by heart:

I flinch ever so slightly to show I've got scruples and morals and I'm not *that* kind of a girl cos you see they don't like *that* kind of a girl these yups, they don't really like any kind of a girl but they do like disguises. Everything nicely wrapped up. So here's where I go all foxy and silent and fight an inner battle that is highly visible (they're thick – you've got to ham it up) and, My Aunty's Knickers, this one turns out to be one of those Who-Hurt-You? merchants and I almost blow the whole job. Gin goes down one lung and out my nose (I'm getting careless, I've had three too many) but still I am an artist so I splutter just in time and turn it into a sort of highly charged sob like he'd hit the nail right on the head. It works. Of course it works. Off he swaggers to the bar with his tight little arse grinning through his chinos and I take a breather.

What's it all about? you wonder. That's what I wonder too sometimes, cos what's a brain like me doing with pricks like him? But then I look at my bank balance and think, come on girl, you're getting there.

What's it all about? you wonder. What d'you think? It's

about sex, like it's always been, 'cept now it's better cos it's about Safe Sex. *I love Safe Sex.*

Now these Johns are so afraid of Aids they won't put it in you and God, what a blessing for the thinking girl. You don't have to take your clothes off. You don't even have to let him into the house (I want you so much John, we might get carried away). All you've got to do is put up with an earful of spit, a load of highly dodgy right-wing conversation and act like you're dying for it – and the last bit's how you get your pressies cos Johns feel guilty about denying it to you. Makes you laugh.

And this is an important bit: Johns *love* romance. They want you to romance them. They get off on all that dark corner bit and putting on a silly business voice when you ring them at home (ring them at home, they love it, ring them in the middle of the night, they thrive on guilt) and they can't get enough of slumming it off the stockbroker belt, Del-boys and cafes, holding hands under tables. And you don't even have to kiss them—tell them you've got mouth ulcers. And what keeps the whole ball rolling is they can't resist telling their mates: 'I'm having an *Affair*' – cos what's the use in being naughty if you've got no one to confess to? And John can pretend he does IT. John is not afraid of AIDS.

Which brings me, horribly, back to John.

Here comes John now, my last John, my grand finale and it's swaying, it thinks it's got it made, it's sort of brimming and relaxed and it doesn't spill a drop, and here comes John now, thank Christ it's my last one, and it's lowering down and

99

watch this smile play on my lower lip, I've got it down to an art it's sort of trembly and yes, it says, I'm all heart, and here comes John now and it's totally pleased, it thinks it's totally safe and listen girls, I am going to take this John for *every* little thing it's got.

Remission

Mick pulls himself up by the window bars of his cell. His biceps bulge weakly. His netted, hair-filled, wide-pored vest strains across his back. The sun shines lemon lollipops of light on his face. Behind him, Warden X leans on the door jamb and exhales great lungfuls of love. 'Visitor for you.'

+

'I think of my little lump,' Lucy tells *Woman's Hour*, hugging her stomach, pausing as the microphone unexpectedly whines, 'as though I'm growing a child. I've decided to nurture it.'

+

'You didn't flipping marry *that*, did you?' Mick sighs in the visiting room, retuning the dial.

Eric sighs too. 'I know, I know . . . But she seemed so, so . . . *doting*.'

She looked nice in his sports car. She had fluffy blonde

hair, a snub nose. She was easily pleased. She tanned evenly. It was difficult to list her attractions now. She liked playing house. If only she would *fade* like a pretty woman.

Lucy has been dying publicly for six years.

'I've only got six months,' she sobbed, six years ago.

A life sentence. The weeks passed . . . years. 'I'm in remission.'

'Tri*ffic*!' said Eric. And rushed to vomit in the sink. In the mirror he froze on the full electronically lit horror of his face.

'Mmm. Who's the fox?' Distant echo: 'Fox . . . fox . . .'

Eric was *so* . . . handsome once, six years ago: ski-tanned, with a tawny lustrous sheen. Now, his eyes have the salmon pink and dotty print of the *Financial Times*. His chest pants rapidly, comically, like a sick dog's. His tongue, involuntarily, lolls out. He swears it wears a short, Daz-white fur coat. 'Fuck! My tongue's wearing a . . .'

'I think she's immortal,' Eric moans. 'I think someone's given her the gift of eternal life. How am I s'posed to get my hands on her money? I mean, I keep hearing this loud thump, thump pulse.'

'Moan, moan, moan,' Mick says. And spits.

+

'I saw Jesus this morning,' Lucy smiles, in the new giant cottage, in the village of Little Hepping, as seen, thrice, in *Hello!* magazine. 'He was standing at the bottom of the bed and the look he gave me was of, so full of love, I mean,' she

giggles, 'I couldn't make an artist's impression of him or anything. What I saw was love. Pure love.'

'Really,' says Eric, and swallows his toast.

He plops a kiss on the air above her pink bald head and
sweeps through the house.

Like an arrow. Through the drive, through the village.
Smudging towns. Into the City, into the bank, up in a sec,
in the see-through lift. He barks into the mobile phone, the
intercom, the Internet, a Dictaphone, his secretary's intri-
cate ear. He makes her earrings jangle freely with nerves.
He stops, fused, and looks, forehead pulsing (a great green
highway down his head), out through the window, at the
opulently tinted pumping sky.

MISERY!

'Lucy's on her way up,' his secretary's Dalek voice grates
through the intercom.

Eric, slowly, batters his forehead back and forth against
the cold violet glass. Far below, the traffic picks at his beat.
He sees himself fall . . . like a Rock of Eric. In ground *rush*.
His nose-breath greys the glass: two sniffy whiffs from a tomb.

'Hello darling,' Lucy yells, 'sur-*pri-ise*!' It is not. She arrives
each lunchtime positively coloured, demanding treats. 'Darling, lunch. I did one hundred and fifty-*five* press-ups today:
feel this.' Eric has to fight the impulse to punch her out.

+

'I'm not just saying this for effect,' Lucy tells her Health
Support Team, 'but since they found it I've felt loads better.

Even . . .' her smile broadens, extends to include her pretty, even back teeth, 'sexy.' Her support team smile, edgily, back.

+

'Wake up, Eric, how do you like . . . *these*.' Twin twiglets in pearly-pink stay-ups.

'Wow,' Eric says, flatly, 'nice.'

In the morning his ears are slopping, wintry-grey, swimming pools of tears.

+

'Me,' Sabine McBrown, his girlfriend, hisses into the phone, 'that's all you ever think about. Me me me.'

Which is true.

Though Eric often thinks: Oh Lord, *why me*?

Who could have predicted the media avalanche over his head? Boulders of print. Character stones, syllables dense and descending, scrolling like grey scale, like black snow . . . The swoop-up of Lucy's cancer star. His MISERY began not with Lucy's terminal news (the mushroom cloud found clamped at the belly of her X-ray) but with her hothouse bloom . . . The chewy *stretch* of her remission. Her face now radiates from magazine racks. The phone rings. It's lawyers, it's agents, producers, breakfast TV. They love her pithy plucky style *so* much. Her face is photogenic, her eyes have the moist appeal of veal, her voice sounds mellifluous, manly even, on the radio. Lucy beams. Her skin blooms the silver hue of fruit.

Uncommissioned, just after the terminal shock news, she

wrote that *one* article for *GET IT! Good Health Magazine*, simply penned, and now, Lucy waves at the moist green lawns, is modest, just *look*. TV lights bleach the lounge. Soon, she's earning commission on her remission. 'Lucy, you have,' her agent affirms, '*fantastic* media viability . . .' An exercise video *Fit to Die. A Cancer Cook Book . . .*

'Great news,' the agent screams, 'Elsbeth Carter's got it. Secondaries. Liver. *You*, Lucy McCann, will soon be the nation's sickest sweetheart.'

'Riff*ic*!' said Eric, as the avalanche fell on his head.

The postman grumbles up the path, lumbagoed out from the loaded fan bags.

+

'She *is* immortal . . .' Eric moans, at his teatime tryst, lying in mushed up bed, in the Red Rope Hotel with Sabine McBrown. 'Why can't she just *hurry up* and die?'

Sabine sits up, with a tremor of her supermodel egg-cup breasts. Her eyes narrow.

'You, Eric, are a selfish . . . *runt*. Lucy has got *cancer*, you know.'

'I *know*,' Eric snaps, twanging on his briefs, '*I* know. She *enjoys* it.'

Outside the Red Rope Hotel, Eric stands flaying, flapping in the steak-house-and petrol-sodden air, trying to crank up. He sees other fellows flying like arrows home. He sniffs his suit-pits and smells Sabine, stinky banknotes . . . death. Bawling in front of his own eyes, thinking, Why, you pathetic *jerk*, he whirls into a phone booth and rings, using his fingers' digital memory, each single friend. No one's in. He rings North Watford, Mick, old mate. But Mick isn't in. He keeps on forgetting. *The inconvenience!* He must wait for visiting time at Her Majesty's pleasure.

In the visiting room, Mick smokes a fag. The fag is the hardest thing in his near-toothless mouth.

'What I regret most,' he says, 'is the years of dental neglect.'

'Yeah,' says Eric, bored. 'What you in for, anyway?'

'Flip me, you ask! You been coming here for, 'ow . . . ? Six, seven, I don't know *years* and *finally* . . . It's all me me me with you. Insider trading if you must . . . Nah, not really. Murder. GBH!'

The idea takes *one* second to form. 'No,' Mick says. 'You've got to be *joking. No* way.'

Eric, as Persuader, has to listen to *a lot* of tales.

'. . . I had a car, me BM dub, or me Roller. Can't remember which one 'cept it was my white one. Parked it outside my house. All the cars used to get done. I gets a dog, one of them evil smiley cunts. I see the kids prowl. I say, Kids leave me car cos I've got this big, BIG Rottweiler in there. I walk away. I hear this one kid whisper, Your dog, mister, she like fire? . . .'

. . . I'm on the bus. I see this bloke and he's looking at me. So I say, You looking at me? And this bloke says, As it happens, I am looking at you. So says, You looking at me . . .'

'Fascinating,' Eric murmurs as the italics sink on. He chews his lip and looks round the smoke-packed snogging room. Apart from a warden staring him down like a wolf, prison life don't seem so bad.

'If you like it up the arse,' Mick says, 'it's great.'

'Why,' Eric says, with their precise grammar-school enunciation, 'are you talking like that?'

'Because,' Mick whispers, 'I'd be dead meat if I talked like me.'

+

Murder, Eric thinks, on the eighth anniversary of Lucy's cancer child. The word expands like a helium-filled balloon in his head, squashes his brain round its billowing bowl. Mercy, much nicer. Like doing her *and* the nation a favour, really.

'Darling, I've made your favourite – mmm, scrummy cottage pie!' Lucy interrupts. A tremor of pain ripples both their lips. A sweet sheet of burnt black meat snags beneath the ceiling, beneath the new and amusing load of gold rococo.

''Rriffic,' says Eric.

Through the French windows, on the smoky grey lawns, he sees slugs on the long haul, stoically trawling their backpacks, leaking viscera . . . Worms fingering up through the soil – giving *him* the finger? Whooping murderously, giving vent, Eric runs around the garden and stamps them out. Panting at the centre of his own blue bloody bootprints, he sees the lawns fissure, go.

'Oh, hold me,' Lucy says, in the night.

No, Eric thinks, hold *me*.

+

'Dying's been so good for me,' Lucy tells the *Gaby Roslin Show*. 'I was just a loving wife before . . . before . . . I feel as though I've just popped into a new dimension.'

'Like, frigging . . .' Eric screams weakly at the TV screen, '*Third*.'

Tears freeze on Lucy's fabulous bones. The cameras choke on all there is to lose: the giant cottage in Little Hepping; the dear-honeyed facade, the prettied privet, a Labrador panting lemony breaths, view of a banker ducking underneath a varnished duck sculpture hedge.

+

'She *is* immortal . . . Micksy, oh, please,' Eric says, squeezing out a tear. 'Please. You're out on parole soon. I don't mean hurt. Just . . .' He searches for a couple of nice harmless words, sees a candle go blank, painless, without sound, 'snuff her.'

'Well, let me think,' Mick says, stroking his jaw. 'In the words of Janet Jackson, "And what have you done for me lately?" I think there's a little accounting to do first . . . we were, I believe, eight, and you sat on my chest and fed me worms.'

'Oh, for *Chrissakes*.'

'. . . *My* Slade album. Slag Allen ended up with it. How? . . .

'. . . In 1978 you bought nil packets of fags, and I bought, look at this paper please, that's right, five billion fags. In . . .'

+

'As you die,' Lucy tells Kilroy – and Oprah – 'you receive the gift of love.'

+

'Why', Eric shouts, 'am I the one getting the *shit* when *she's* the one doing the dying?'

'. . . The time you borrowed fifty quid and disappeared for three years. The time you refused to appear for the defence as it would damage your flipping career. The time, after Reading, you told me to ask for a Peter Gabriel haircut.'

'Please,' Eric begs. 'I'm begging ya.'

'Why ja *marry* her if you can't *stand* her?'

'I know, I know . . .' Eric weighs up two palm-loads of air. 'All I ever wanted,' he says, lying, '*ever*, is a giant cottage, a blonde. Maybe some kiddies.' Pots of cash. Power. A classy *new* Barbie doll every four years.

'Yeah, well, ditto,' Mick says, also lying, winking an infinitesimal eyelid at Warden X. Warden X expands by the door, he damn near implodes with love.

+

'Lucy's coming up,' says the Dalek. Eric, internally, groans. Lucy enters, floats in beneath a flotilla of gold helium balloons. They fizz all over the room. They fart.

'Aren't they just so *sensational*!' she crows. 'So cheering! I got them from a fan . . . Oh, hello everyone.'

Eric mouths behind a grey bank of backs: '*I* am in a *meeting, Lucy.* A *meeting!*' He stabs, with his tiepin, at a passing helium balloon. '*My*', stab, 'life.'

The big bang sends Lucy out in a head-first, thoughtful skid across the parquet floor. Into the papers. Into a rift. Into a new glossy five-book deal: 'Save Your Life; Now *Save* Your Marriage.'

The lift takes Eric down.

+

'The time you sold my car for me, ha ha . . .

' . . . when you borrowed my Wrangler shirt and I never got it back . . .

'When my mum died and you couldn't be arsed . . .'

'The Liverpool away, when you snogged Nancy Michelson in the Kop *throughout* the match.'

'When you don't phone,' says Sabine. 'When you talk about yourself all the time. When I have to do all the work. When you just lie there floppy like a girl.'

'Mr McCann, we're leaving,' his PA, secretary, and five of his clients say in a block. They leave trailing insults and adjectives: 'Insufferable . . . arrogance, crap, bastard, can't even . . . add . . .'

+

'Please Mick, I'll give you . . .'

'Can't hear you,' Mick hums, humming. 'Gone deaf.'

'FIFTY THOUSAND POUNDS!'

+

Down.

'Leave me,' Eric whimpers at various satellite shows, 'alone.' Eric sees *her* face on the cover of the *TV Times*.

On the *Pearl and Dean Show*.

Cars drive through Little Hepping at dawn and whisk it away to studios in Birmingham.

Lucy sits up in pancake make-up, her smile brave. She makes the studio audience laugh.

They stand and cheer.

She wins a modelling contract from a famous London wig-maker, beams across towns. She looks, Eric thinks, with her pap-white raised ankles and knees, like a twig in a wig . . .

'Leave me alone,' Eric sobs, pressing his palms to the side of his head, hard. Implode, bastard head.

'What's wrong with it?' Sabine asks in the Red Rope Hotel, peering into Eric's lap.

'It's spineless,' Eric moans, 'it's snuffed.'

The postman staggers up the path.

. . . Men's groups fax regular letters of support. Short stories arrive describing different ways to grieve. Strangers drag Eric further down with pitiful looks. An old lady on the train home bawls, tears pellet off her cheeks. Eric and the old lady sit on the train and scream.

'Fuck,' Eric groans in his sleep, filling his ears up with tears. 'Fuck pulse, bollocks, fuck.'

Down.

The manager of the Red Rope Hotel steps briskly out from his storeroom cupboard to personally humiliate and deliver a short British shrift: 'For shame, your sick and lovely lady wife . . .' Eric arm-wrestles for the room key.

Sabine sobs, 'You're really such a bastard, Eric.'

'But you know I can't *stand* her.'

'She's got *cancer*!'

Cancer cancer fuck fuck.

Sabine whispers, 'Eric, what if the papers find out?' Her face turns ugly with fear.

+

'Mick, sixty thousand . . . sixty-five.'

+

He shoots up to the office in the morning with a skiddy stink of burning rubber. He shoots up the lift shaft. In the board-room, above the mahogany table, he sees, as though through a funhouse mirror, his shirt distorted, his wavering sideburns. A giant green pulse beating down the centre of his skull. Thump, thump pulse.

'Lucy's on her way up.' Urgh.

Lucy enters wearing a dress shrivelled like a sleeve. 'I just bought it,' she cries, holding the wrinkles out wide. 'Guess how much.'

Eric guesses.

'No, Eric. It was . . .' (distant echo) '*ous*and *ous*and pounds.'

+

'I feel,' Eric says, loosening his collar, 'as though I'm wearing a metal head. Please,' he begs. 'It's not like you're going to heaven, Mick, is it? I'll pay you,' he whispers, shifting a decimal point, 'once the insurance kicks in, one hundred thousand pounds.'

'Think about it,' Mick says, stroking his jaw. 'I must admit, she is pretty sickening.'

Outside the prison, Eric leaps and punches air.

+

The surgeon says, 'Mrs McCann, I've never seen anything like this. It's, er, completely gone.'

Lucy screams, snatches at her cleared X-ray, 'What do you *mean* ger-*gorn* . . . ?'

'I suppose,' the surgeon says, rabbit-faced, 'there may have been some . . . er . . . frightful mix-up.'

'What is,' snaps the agent, 'this *gorn*?'

+

Warden X holds Mick's hand. 'I don't want you to go.'

'I imagine,' Mick says, stroking stubble, 'I'll be back here shortly.' He kisses Warden X full in the throat.

+

Eric lands in red rain. 'Strange.' (Distant echo: '... Strange ... strange'.) His arms stretch and, far below, he sees his hands touch the pavement, rather delicately. A red bomb. A pulmonary embolism. 'What about,' Eric says, dying, *my fucking remission!*'

'Oh,' says Lucy's soundbite, 'this is an immense personal loss.'

+

The trees make a sound like distant applause. The pale tulips on the funereal path stand like spoons. The soil turns in a rich, moist Christmas-cake mix. Eric sinks straight into the ground. At the impact, everyone, astonished, cries. Lucy sobs because her career in cancer has now been extended by one in grief. Her agent howls as there is really only so-so mileage in Miracles and Mix-ups. Sabine bawls because there is now less chance of being smudgily reproduced by the *News of the World*. Mick tears up because, though Eric was a selfish old git, he was still his good old North Watford mate. Warden X cries because Mick in civvies – he just looks so goddamn *sweet*?

As the sods hit the lid Eric thinks, 'Oh, why Lord. Why *me*?' The early worms begin their tunnel down. Distant echo: 'Me ... me ... me me ...'

Nerve Endings

The sprout of the nerve is a delicious pain: like a bit lip, or a mouth ulcer the tongue seeks out. It sprouts gradually and then ruffles invisibly.

In middle age she was covered in fine sensate fur.

But, there were pullulating decades to go before then.

Newly single, she found she enjoyed the tap-down search at airports and at quaysides, at the end of red lanes, even when she had nothing to declare. She became skilled at attracting a certain trained uniform attention: she went blink-less like a terrorist. Or she blushed. She did not invite a full naked body search. Rather, it was the sweep of hands under her arms she enjoyed; the T-bar search they made of her skin. She felt an empathy with, and was touched by, the little port-able metal-detecting machine: it cried out, like her, at every single scrape of metalloid skin. 'Touch *me*!'

Later, she relied on the circle of rejection and skin-tingling renewal.

When Philip left she found it was the back of her neck that

became most affected. The nerve endings there were raw. She had her long wavy red hair styled in a way that required a regular precision cut: a snippy, close-necked shave. Mack, the hairdresser, had such long warm fingers, cool fingernails. He blew the hair-dust from her neck with professional distaste: she saw it spray back in the mirror like shorn red grass. His breath sent her mad. Her spine shrivelled with pleasure and stayed coiled for a month. Blue nerves arrowed up her bloodstream, shot through like scissor blades. The nerves on her neck waved. Inevitably, as Mack's cut took on a more deliberate and erotic edge – he made moves behind her like a belly dancer – she became, swiftly, turned off.

She often had a boyfriend (for she was pretty, young, leisured, rich . . .) but, after the first all-over body contact, the first surge of excitement (Touch *me*!) it was as if her nerve endings burrowed back down under her skin and died.

She was called all manner of negative names.

When Andrew left – leaving behind a jungle scrawl, a padded rubber-leafed carpet (he'd filed down all her house plants) – she found it was her right breast that craved attention. Not the nerve centre of the nipple but the right-hand side. Two inches of green-veined flesh. She found herself crushed on public transport, both hands up clutching the hard red plastic strap, a man or old woman, student or tourist, it did not matter whom (though if they were beautiful it added fizz to her *frisson*) pressed to her side. She swung from the train ceiling, round and round the Circle Line, her breast throbbing swoon.

She went through boyfriends like lunch. They were met with an astonishing gobbling passion. Early on in the relationship though, she inspired the reverse: the most passionate and vengeful rejections. She was accused of usury. Negation. All manner of negative names.

Uncoupled, she was affected like a hothouse flower on a rotating plinth. The sun hit her this way and that way, another day, another way; and she'd sprout hungry tendrils of feeling. Buds. Tiny waxy pink mouths screaming: *touch!*

When Colin left (after tipping a fruit cocktail over her head, after snapping her favourite red-gold lipstick), she found it was the tip of her nose that tingled. She made appointments at private clinics, she went for private consultations. Medical men, face decorators, touched and drew her nose. They measured it with a burning slide rule. Her eyes, they noted, in code, were dilated. She sniffed continuously. A severe cocaine addiction would explain a lot. They'd cut the cartilage, operate anyway.

When Paddy left (he fed her goldfish chilli powder), she found it was her toes that demanded to be crushed under strangers' boots, or slipped into shoe after shoe at shoe stores. Her ankle was, later, pleasured in this way too, by ankle chains in a sequence of ankle-chain fitting rooms.

At times, when she had a new boyfriend, and they walked arm in arm through smoky russet city parks, and floppy dogs bounced around them, or they knotted fingers together or made lace that way in pubs, or kissed in tunnel-black alleys, she thought this more ordinary sensation was certainly good enough.

But they would leave.

After many years, after much analysis, it was decided, it was *realized*, it was she who sent them away.

It was the casual traffic of touch that did for her. Money pressed into her palm; a wrist-bone knocking against her own; feeling someone strange steer the base of her spine through a carnival crowd, then disappear.

It could not be bought in an obvious and carnal way, though in times of touch-drought, or when the place affected tingled, as if it would blossom into gigantic garland sores (Touch, touch *me*!) she'd employ a masseur – with a husband's (fleeting) sense of shame. But, it was not exactly the same.

When Mel, in an effort to win her back, sent a gaudy bank of flowers, hairy, tropical shoots, it was the flower boy's pen knocking against her knuckles which threw her back on the couch. When Mel arrived her hunger seemed deranged.

She never knew where the next nerve would come.

It was Frank who affected her eyelashes and sent her fluttering to a doctor, who combed them, his face lunar-huge, and stared at her blank-eyed. Her eyelashes were certainly a little . . . sparse, he said, picking one out, but he had no real explanation for this. She did. It was a favourite trick of hers to glue an eyelash to her cheek. Men, she found, loved to lift or blow it off. She felt their coloured breaths on her skin.

Tobacco-coloured, mint . . . She'd enjoyed many such tender displays.

She went to France often to have her cheeks briskly kissed by strangers. This hunger was never assuaged.

In Italy, after John (he'd cut the labels from all her designer-labelled clothes), as she walked in the warm yellow air, she felt her left elbow activate. In Italy she allowed the sons of waiters to tout it to tablecloth after tablecloth. While the elbow throbbed, she grew immensely fat.

In Ireland, after Mark (after he'd unstrung her uncultured pearls, hurled them from the balcony), thin again, her forehead made demands and creased up. It broke out in tears. The manager of the hotel sent for hot wet hankies and stroked her forehead down. He was alarmed by her delirium but, once he'd bent to kiss her, it passed.

As she aged her skin grew more clamorous and thickly coated with nerve fur. She fell over often and had to be helped up. She dropped her keys abruptly, her diamond rings, her credit cards and so was often pleasantly and rudely bumped. She found herself, with a little start of surprise, crushed in a taxi in Mexico City with families and extended families of sheep. A sheep or a peasant breathed heat in her ear. She felt, at the right delicious pressure point, a wool-rimmed, spam-pink, rushing slab of tongue.

When she was too old to attract boyfriends she found, to her relief, that she no longer required the kick-start of rejection. Her skin forgot their names. Her skin fur swayed as tall as corn. The centre of feeling still moved mysteriously over her body and imprinted itself variously, like corn circles. Her ears demanded. Her little toes. The shine on her shin bones.

She began to seek more and more comfort in the medical profession. It was expensive. Her list of private consultations was awesome and crossed the carpet into little red ante-rooms. Her hypochondria advanced. It galloped across continents. One time it was a fork of green vein on her chest. The pulse there alarmed her. Another time it was a tiny freckle in her eyebrow, another in her groin. Another . . . Once she was arrested for lewd behaviour and once she was sent to a drying-out clinic and forced to follow a twelve-step recovery programme. She did not recover. She became an embarrassment to the remnants of her family and friends. A drag on the family's dwindling purse strings. She'd demand intimate touch from strangers, voicing her need out loud: Lay your little finger on my tongue. Touch my skull, honey. Touch me *here*. But the nurses said she was a lovely old lady. She enjoyed, in so far as she never once complained, her bed bath. When they took her pulse or blood pressure, put a finger to her wrist, or stethoscope to her heart, pumped up her upper arm, her face wore a look of such radiant sweetness. When she died she died twice: the first time she simulated death in order to feel a finger and thumb press upon her eyelids. The nurses were startled and then pretty pissed off.

The next time she died was also the first time.

I'm Running Late

It started off like a normal Saturday really.

I told my mum if John rang or Andy or Eddie or Gary I wasn't in. My mum said, 'You're old enough to do your own dirty work.' I said, 'Well, I won't answer it.' My dad joined in, yelling up the stairs, 'So how many boyfriends has Lady Muck got *now*?' I said, 'In my day . . .'

He said, 'In my day, we only had one . . .'

I said, all shocked, '*You* had a boyfriend, Dad?'

Mum came in with the extension lead while I was diffusing my hair. 'What a surprise, Tina, it's for you.' I gave her my look. I said, 'Ooh . . . you-wouldn't-let-it-lie.' I snatched the phone. I said, 'If that's you John Buckley you can piss right off,' but it wasn't John it was Sandy. Sandy, my mate.

She was crying. I heard her go, 'Oh, Tina,' then she got taken over by a sob and the phone crashed down. What a drama queen. When I'd done my make-up and got a decent side parting I rang her back. I said, 'Oh no, really . . . did ja? . . . no! . . . would you believe it . . . bloody right!' But

I couldn't really listen as – with the curtains drawn and the lamp on the floor shining up into my mirror – my teeth looked really yellow. I went and drew back the curtains, switched off the light and what a relief, it was just a funny shadow. I picked up the phone again. Sandy was still bawling, '. . . it's not fair, I only did it once . . . and you know I can't stand needles . . . and oh God *hospitals* . . .' I said, 'Eh?' I thought, Oh-oh, silly cow's preggers. She was off again so I said, 'Look I'm running a bit late today Sandy but, Sandy, Sandy *listen* . . .' and I arranged to meet her in the arcade for a coffee and a proper chat-ette, cheer her up.

I had to go there anyway to get some new leggings for tonight.

When my dad dropped me off on the high street I was a couple of minutes early so I popped into Next (it's really gone down), and, when I was sure no one I know would see me, I dived into What She Wants and bought the leggings and a top that looks like silk but ain't.

By the time I get to the arcade I'm running a bit late and I see Sandy through the crowd by the telephone hoods looking well pissed off so I look like I've got the hump too so she won't say nothing. She's wearing pink Catwoman sunglasses, and a stone-washed fashion mistake. Trainers. I note them but I don't say nothing. Me, I wear black.

Sandy wants to 'talk' first, more like 'sob', but I go, 'Later love,' and pat her hand. 'Let's liven this place up a bit, God it is boring. Look how bored people are. Bored. BORING.' Sandy goes, 'Let's shop,' getting into it, and I go, 'Yeah, till we drop.' We go into Our Price first to have a look at their new boy (ugly), then The Accessory Shop. Sandy buys a pink bum-bag and a matching baseball cap and I buy a really *special* Mexican necklace and a pair of really delicate silver filigree earrings. At the counter it's obvious, the difference between us.

When we come out though we have a right laugh. We see this – nerd we went to school with, Ronnie Boyle, dressed up as the security guard in a big brown uniform, looking well dodgy. When he sees us his lips go, 'Oh no,' and all the colour drains from his spots. It was really funny right. He sort of sidestepped into these potted trees. Sandy goes, 'Ooh, isn't that, er, *Ronnie Boyle*,' and I go, 'Nah,' studying my nails, 'it's a big lump of dogshit.' We follow him up and we follow him down the arcade and Sandy's calling out, 'Pin-head boily, boily boily pus-head.' And I'm going, 'Cor, hasn't he grown a nice bum, Sandy. It's got really tight.' We march behind him like Nazis, Sieg-heiling and talking in loud voices about all the shops we're going to rob and all these bored people are well happy now and Ronnie Boyle is dead miserable and Sandy's going, 'Tina. If you forgot that Semtex again . . .' I almost wet my knickers. We let him off by the fountain going, 'See ya next week then, Ronnie.'

They're piping in some of Bananarama's Greatest and we sway to that for a while and dance about as we have our fags. Then Sandy thinks she sees Sister Emelda, a nun from our old school, dressed up in a leather coat and silver leggings with dyed black nylony hair, just like the hair on my old My

Little Pony. There is a *bit* of a resemblance. The hair goes into Boots and we follow her, ducking and diving behind the counters, to see if she's going to buy any 'sanitary protection gals'. That's Sandy's imitation. Sometimes Sandy's deadly boring but sometimes she's a right laugh.

We go into McDonald's. I get the coffee and some chips and Sandy takes off her sunglasses and her eyes are squinty and in slits. She goes, 'Oh, Tina,' and her head is right down there on the table like it weighs a ton. I let her cry for a bit even though it's deadly embarrassing right and she's really showing me up. Every now and again I say, 'That's right, let it out, love,' and pat her hand. I've smoked two more fags by the time she's decent. Down the next booth, though, there's these three boys, leather jackets, and one of them thinks he's God's gift and starts imitating Sandy and the thing is, it's really funny, I mean he was a really good mimic, like Rory Bremner, but of course I can't laugh even though it's hurting my lips not to. While Sandy's recovering and putting on her make-up though I go right over and tell them to piss off out of it. The other two are nothing special but this Rory Bremner one, he's all right, so I look at him when I say it and the other two are going, 'Ooh-wa, ooh-wa,' really juvenile, and this Rory Bremner one looks me up and then looks me down and just says, really low, 'Open your coat,' and it was really embarrassing, I blushed. When I got back to the table Sandy had her glasses back on and it's odd when people wear dark glasses indoors because it's like they're blind and deaf. She was OK but a bit gulpy and her nose was a bit disgusting. She said this really stupid thing though. She said, 'It's funny to think I won't be around,' and I thought that was really just typical drama queen talk because she'd only have to be in a clinic for an afternoon. To take her mind off it I told her some things about the girls at work and more about this one girl, Patsy, who's got really long hair and knows it so she's always lifting it up like it's deadly heavy and oh-so luxurious and I tell her what Patsy was wearing all last week and that makes Sandy laugh. Then I tell her how this same girl, Patsy, and this other girl she's always going on about, 'my model friend', 'my friend the model' Murial, a right dog, when I went out with them last night and Murial saw her boyfriend in Cheers with this other girl. It was bloody funny. When I finish Sandy laughs but then the laugh turns into crying again, as I've obviously hit a nerve. I said, lying, 'Oh, come on, Sandy, it won't hurt,' and these boys and the Rory Bremner one comes up and it's really funny right because this Rory one starts pretending he's a doctor and tries to take Sandy's pulse and he puts on this Swedish accent and the other two boys are being like robot nurses and I must admit it did really crack me up, though I did tell them to piss right off. Sandy gets up and tries to run to the loo but one of the boys trips her up, a bit, for a joke, and she sort of falls flat on her face and when she gets up one of the lenses from her Cat-woman sunglasses is missing and she doesn't seem to know it so she looks really funny. She runs to the loo and when she's gone this Rory boy suddenly goes into The Fonz and starts calling me Babe and orders his mates to wait for him outside so they go outside and they're acting like bodyguards with their arms folded high up on their chests and he puts his arm round me and goes all Italian calling me Bella bella and I go, all thick, 'No, it's Tina tina actually.' So Sandy comes back and I say, 'Excuse me, kind sir,' but he won't let me out – for ages.

When I look up Sandy's just outside the door and these two boys are messing about a bit, pretending everything's in slow motion and pushing Sandy at each other and going, 'Whoops, whoop-sy,' and Sandy's ponytail is coming undone, she looks a right mess and she's blubbering again. One of them gets her from behind and holds her and the other one starts tickling her round the waist, a little bit rough. Anyway, this Rory boy starts lighting up all my fags and pretending like he can give them up any-time-he-wants, and he's got them in his nose and in his ears and a couple of girls on the next table are going, 'Look at that wanker,' but they start laughing as well. Some boys don't need much encouragement. Soon, right, he's on top of the table pretending to be Elvis Presley and singing into a ketchup bottle and it's really good and me and these two other girls pretend to be backing singers going, 'oo oo oo oo,' and swimming backwards. It was such a laugh. I mean really. Then me and these two girls pretend to be crazy fans and rush at his legs going, 'ELVIS, YOU'RE ALIVE!' Well, I'm going, 'ELVIS, YOU'RE ALIVE,' these two other girls, they're going, 'ELVIS, YOU'RE A WANKER,' but he loves it anyway and soon he's being Tom Jones with a fist down his knickers and a hungry Bob Geldof but the best one was his Jason Donovan on drugs. When the manager comes out with his staff I leg it.

There's no sign, typical, of Sandy and I'm running a bit late. Then I see quite a big crowd over by the fountain, quite a commotion. I think I hear Sandy's voice going, 'Help me, help me,' but I can't be sure as it's a bit noisy. I go to the loo, do my lips and scrunch my hair. The side parting looks really good, even though I say so myself. Then I go to the jewellers to see if they've got this new watch strap in. They ain't. When I get out of there I'm lighting up when Ronnie Boyle lurches past, pulling his portable phone out like it's a gun. When he sees me he stops dead and this big smirk stretches all his spots. I sort of know then. It'll be Sandy. Sandy, showing me up. He goes, and he's well pleased, 'Tina, wanna see something lovely? Over 'ere, by the fountain?' I give him the finger, pushing in the crowd, but even so when I saw what I saw, my jaw dropped.

She's only drowning in the fountain. The two leather jackets are in the fountain up to their knees in splashy water, with Sandy, my mate. They're playing to the crowd, lowering her head in and out like it's a yo-yo. Her shirt was right up round her neck, so it was bloody lucky she was wearing a body. I roll my eyes; it could only happen to Sandy. This little kid next to me is going, 'Daddy I *can't see!*' so the kid gets lifted up and the kid's going, 'I can see now, dunker dunker,' and everybody goes, 'Dunk Her Dunk Her,' and they're dunking Sandy in the water. She's soaking wet already. The funny thing is, Sandy isn't screaming or crying or struggling, nothing. When

I can see her face it's just – blank. Ronnie Boyle is standing on the rim of the fountain laughing, swinging the phone and his cap's right at the back of his head. His other hand conducts the crowd. Anyway, the boys do this yo-yo routine for a few minutes and everybody is chanting and I'm going, 'Hey, leave her alone,' but I can't really get heard. Then the two girls from McDonald's are next to me and one of them goes, 'Isn't that your mate?' and I say, 'Yeah,' and it was nerves really, but I laughed. The next thing I know they're in the fountain as well and I thought they were going to do something really funny right because they both bow to the crowd but then – one of them kicks this boy in the face, whips round and knees the other boy in the balls. The other girl sort of flicks her fingers under this other boy's chin and he collapses in the water. It was amazing. And they didn't seem to mind getting wet either. These two boys crawl over the rim of the fountain onto the floor and start crawling towards the arcade doors. It was all over in a second and except for fountain noise and Bananarama piping out and this little kid still singing, 'Dunker dunker,' it was deadly quiet. They carried Sandy out and her head and arms were lolling backwards. This big space was cleared for her. I sort of couldn't breathe. This picture comes into my mind of Sandy in the school playing-fields imitating Sister Emelda and another of Sandy in the dinner hall starting off a food fight. Before I know what I'm doing I'm screaming, 'SANDY SANDY WAKE UP,' and one of the girls yells to Ronnie Boyle, 'Hey, fuckwit, that better be an ambulance you're calling.' I'm on my knees by this time and I'm rubbing Sandy's hand. One of these girls pushes me out of the way and starts giving Sandy the kiss of life. I start blubbering. Me! I see me and Sandy in Debenham's trying on the wigs and both of us wetting our knickers. Then this other girl whacks me across the face and tells me to shut the fuck up and I shudder to a halt. Then, Sandy opens her eyes and looks straight at me, sort of through me, like she don't know me, turns her head and vomits up all this green water and bits of chips. The ambulance man and a woman come and they put Sandy in a chair, strap her down and carry her off. Then the woman ambulance driver comes back with red blankets and wraps them around these two girls. She puts her arms round them. Everybody is looking at me like I done something. Somehow I get out into the high street. At the ambulance the driver says to me, 'Are you coming?' and – it was nerves really. I looked at my watch. 'Oh,' I said, 'I can't, I'm running a bit late.'

When I got home I fell on my bed and cried and cried. Then I looked in the mirror: oh no, *centre* parting.

We Do Not Forward
Suicide Notes

He took a page from his brand new notepad and wrote down the positives. He wrote:

1). *Today is the start of a journey and I am happy.*
2). *I have just enjoyed* (although 'enjoyed' did not quite cover the tussle on the footpath) *a brisk sea walk and a stimulating conversation with a dear friend.*
3). *Now I will have something nutritious in this . . .*

He looked around, at the other tables hunched under their waxy dark green tablecloths. He had the slight, but vivid impression, the tables, the tables and the chairs, were inching their way to the door, to the cliffs outside. The rocks.

He looked at his first sentence. *I am happy.*

Was this true?

Outside it was raining like it was raining spit. Sea and sky the colour of a prison blanket. He was certainly happy to be inside.

Inside it was warm, at least. And there were long tubes of sugar. And if he wanted chips he could have them.

He crossed out happy and wrote *at peace*. Then he stole a look at the girl who sat an acre away behind the counter.

An ancient striplight sizzled above her head. In the vast, dimly lit and derelict cafe, she was powerfully illuminated like an actress on a stage.

He wrote *I think I will call her Sumi. A Goddess. One day, will I call her girlfriend?*

The girl, whose name was not Sumi, sat staring down at a sheet of paper on which she had written NO UNEVEN SLICES OF TOAST. She had ink from the pen on her stubby fingers. She was smoking a foreign, fast-burning cigarette. He thought she looked Eastern European, from far, far away across the sea, via airports. Maybe Poland. He had heard the Poles liked the seaside. They were hard-working. They liked fairground rides. And vodka.

That was as much as he knew about the Poles.

He wrote *find out more about the poles.*

He studied the girl, pen poised.

She had a large head.

You couldn't help noticing how large the head was. This

might have been because of her hair, which was cropped and dyed a blue-black and stood up on its electric ends, as though a balloon had recently passed over her. Also, she had a long face like a horse has a long face. Tiny tiny tiny eyes. She had not smiled when he'd entered. He wrote *teeth?* He could see the colour of her bra through her shirt. Red. He wrote *cerise*.

—You want something?

—Tea, he said. His voice came out higher than he liked.

She jabbed a thumb at a wall covered in peeling notices, old and new.

He read, beside a laden coat rack, DIE IN YOUR COATS.

DON'T SHOUT I SPEAK ENGLISH.

PAY BEFORE YOU GO.

He frowned, confused.

—You have to pay in advance.

—OK, he said.

—I bring.

She stood up, carrying a pot of stewed tea. She rounded the corner of the counter.

He gaped.

She was huge.

No. Not all over. The head was large, yes, as noted but still within the bounds of, he swallowed, normality. No. He wrote rapidly as she lumbered towards him. *It is as though the bottom half of an obese woman has been attached to the upper half of a slender one. Make this sentence more elegant.*

This explained, he thought, as she aimed the tea into his cup, why the tables were set so far apart.

—You eat?

He stared at her. He nodded, coming to. And lied.

—I'm waiting for a friend.

Although the friend had died forty-six minutes ago.

—Your friend, he eat?

—Yes, we will eat, when my friend gets here.

—Cos otherwise I close. Cos the weather is . . . She pointed at the window which was smeary with grey, and rattled, as though someone, at irregular intervals, were throwing handfuls of gravel at it.

—Shit.

—Right. Shit. Got it.

He watched her walk away. She wore an outsized pale blue tracksuit on her – astonishing – lower half made from a sheeny material which was so thin and stretched in places it was almost net, and inside it, inside it her flesh rolled like seasickness.

She said, without turning.

—I will put the oven on.

He picked up his pen. He wrote rapidly, sweating. He did not like surprises or shocks. *Name: Colin Dexter. Henceforth . . . Henceforth my name is Colin . . . Colin Fletcher and I am safe. I am safe in a cafe beside the* (he thought for a moment) *Atlantic and these are the things I am. Out-going.*

Thrifty. Tidy. Descriptive. I can keep up a correspondence. I can meditate. I am punctual. I am still young. I have seventeen GCSEs. I have a wallet containing forty-seven pounds fifty in my pocket. And credit cards, though not my own.

I am not afraid. I am not afraid.

His pen shook. He thought of his mentor, the Reverend Steerforth, dead now, surely, his spare biro rammed in the side of his neck, still wearing a look of disappointment and surprise at this unexpected end to their day trip. Two looks. If he could talk, what would he say? Pull out the negatives. And? Face them.

The woman's lower half is huge but this should not make me afraid. *We are all animals clinging with our hooves*, no that is not helping, *clinging with our FINGERS, slender fingers, to . . . to the long green grass of the planet.*

The planet turned round. He thought he was going to vomit.

He wrote. *Colin Dexter.* He wrote the worst things about himself. Face them.

I have just got out of prison.

I am short.

The girl came out of the kitchen holding up a platter on which three bound lobsters twitched.

—You choose, she said.

He gulped. He gulped because of their underwear colours,

like bloody laundry, and he gulped because the lobsters reminded him of? Himself. This was difficult to explain.

A note wouldn't do. He drew a sketch of a lobster and wrote ME next to it and an arrow pointing down.

—You choose, she said.

He chose the smallest one.

—My favourite, Sumi said. I cook now.

He followed her into the kitchen, padding in her shadow, with the intention of doing her harm. He would puncture her and she would deflate like the Reverend Steerforth. He thought of the good Reverend deflating on the cliff face, spread out under the night sky, as though wide awake but really not, raindrops splashing the blue colour from his eyes. Later, he supposed, he would have to bury him, then track back to the car park and take care of the car. Otherwise? Helicopters. I failed you, Reverend Steerforth, he thought. I am not, after all, he felt his throat thicken with – premature – remorse, capable of love or, he drew his hand back the better to stab the girl, a suitable candidate for day release. Sumi turned round. She looked at the fork clenched in his hand. She looked at him. They listened to the water bubble on the stove. Then Sumi took the fork from him – the strange thing was he *let her* – and speared the lobster into the pot.

—They scream, she said. It is upsetting but it is over quickly.

—Yes, he said. For he did know that.

The lobster screamed once, faintly, like a girl in a park.

*

—Elizabetha, she said, in the silence that followed.

—Colin.

—Tonight, she said, Colin, I invite you to eat. For free.

Colin and Elizabetha sat at a table at the centre of the vast and derelict cafe. In front of them three candles, rammed into ketchup bottles, threw a bronzed and trembling sheen over the feast. Colin looked about him, trying to commit the scene to memory. The lobsters slid a little on their burnished field of lettuce. Some hundred yards away a Black Forest gateau revolved slowly in a green lit-glass cabinet. The cafe smelt of cooked lobster and burnt-out plugs. And outside the wind blew and shook the window frames and rustled the notices along the walls. Perhaps, Colin thought, if I find myself once more incarcerated (as does seem likely), in a prison cell, I will recall this most perfect of nights. Taking his cue from the girl he tucked a napkin decorated with ancient reindeers under his chin. He picked up his pen and wrote, *I feel strangely at peace with this giant – unblinking – girl. Will we live happily ever after?*

—Tonight, the girl said, reaching for a lobster, she lowered her huge head so their eyes met, she lowered her voice so he could barely hear her, I . . .

She said something he couldn't quite catch.

—What?

—I kill myself.

He was so surprised his hand took notes. She spoke quickly, gesturing with a claw to the windows churning with weather.

He wrote:

E intends to fling herself off cliff face. Fuck.

Reason? E has watched many customers do this . . .

Question: Is suicide contagious? Will find out.

Revelation: Explains coat rack and limited menu.

First E tries to help . . . She talks. They talk. All night, talk . . . They eat her . . . business . . . Ruined. They use her pen to write their suicide notes.

They jump anyway. They fucking jump.

Elizabetha sucked meat between her teeth. He rested with her. Then she went on.

He wrote. *E now so fucking depressed she eats.*

Explains: Gigantism. But now E knows they have right idea. Convinced she will feel no pain. This is because E has drunk many painkillers not because fat ass will protect against rocks. Now, all E feels is . . . hungry.

They ate. The girls's appetite was enormous. Colin chewed his food slowly, pushing his portions towards her, because he didn't want the meal to end. He watched Elizabetha's mouth chomping through the lobster meat; a shine gather on her horse jaw, gloves of silver grease build on her hands so her black chipped nail varnish glistened. He saw his tiny self reflected in her tiny tiny tiny eyes. At the end of the meal Elizabetha burped grandly.

—Now, she said, I ready.

She lumbered to the door and flung it open. She was nearly knocked back by the wind. Above her head a couple of seagulls flashed their silver undersides.

—Nooo, Colin said, before he knew he would say anything.

He had time to note this new sensation: he had never wanted someone to *live* before.

—Give me one reason, Elizabetha said, not turning round, why not?

—Because . . . Colin said. He thought of all the reasons he had heard why life should be allowed to just go on . . . And? None of them would do. A green phosphorous light strobed his boots . . . and he had it.

—Because you haven't had your pudding yet!

Elizabetha nodded, this was true.

Closer inspection of the Black Forest gateau revealed a terminal disease. Colin ransacked the cupboards and found wrinkled bags of banana-flavoured Angel's Delight. He sat on Elizabetha's lap and fed her yellow teaspoons. I am feeding her sunshine, he thought. She smiled sleepily, showing him a tongue so grooved he thought, in his erotic stupor, I could lay my palm in it. My whole head. Maybe even my . . . Elizabetha's eyes began to roll. He had to twang her cerise bra strap to wake her. Hey, he said. Wake up. He said, the only thing he could say. Something he had never said to another human before.

*

—Elizabetha, will you dance?

They danced to a Christmas compilation tape he found at the back of a drawer snappy with mousetraps, turning together at the same speed as the Black Forest gateau; Colin's head pressed into Elizabetha's solar plexus; her giant chin resting on his bald spot: one cerise breast, heavy as a post-bag, on each of his shoulders. They turned until the windows ran with their condensation and the candles burned down to their ketchupped socks. When the jingle bells gave their last tinkle, Elizabetha lifted Colin up like a child and kissed him. It was the sweetest kiss, tasting of sugared banana sandwiches from long ago. *Am I happy?* Colin thought, feet swinging. *Am I?* He opened his eyes. It took him a few moments to recognize the face, pale as the moon, pressed against the black window, a face familiar from visiting hours, bloodless lips mouthing, not homilies this time, just the two words: HELP . . . ME.

Three words: HELP ME COLIN.

The Reverend Steerforth.

So.

Not dead after all.

Elizabetha followed his gaze. Her expression hardened.

—Another one, she said. She pointed at a notice he couldn't read on the wall.

—NO, she yelled, MORE TIME WASTERS. She dropped Colin and opened the door. Before he could stop her, did he want to stop her? To his joy, he found that yes, yes he did! He grabbed his pen, as Elizabetha hauled the Reverend Steerforth over her shoulder and – at a run – despatched him into the inky blue blackness beyond the cliff.

You were right, Colin wrote rapidly and faster than a man could fall, *you were right to befriend me after all, my dear Reverend Steerforth, your faith in me was justified because look at me now. Look at me. At last I feel your love.*